Almost His

James Bettington

Contents

Chapter 1

A smile graces my face, a soft one filled with a shy background as my eyes scan the small group of people around me. As the music plays on, laughter and cheers filling the air, I stand away from the noise and applause, watching from above as the party unravels before my eyes. While couples dance to the music, people taking pictures to post or remember the event by, individuals drinking from the punch, and a few girls rush to the bathroom due to a dress malfunction or heartbreaking event, I watch from above. I feel like Gatsby, in control of the situation as I simply monitor what goes on, not allowing myself to become part of the mess down below.

The hotel that the prom is hosted in is the same as the last three held here. The massive ballroom in the hotel is spacious to say the least, wooden flooring, cream walls decorated for the senior class of this year, and the five chandeliers in the room simply here for the ostentatious look. Teenagers like myself fill the massive ballroom to the limit, the balcony overlooking the majority of the dance floor even crowded with people. However, the people up here are more my speed, rather watching and taking in the event rather than participating and facing the consequences of a twisted ankle or heartbreak.

"Having fun?" A voice calls out behind me, soft yet filled with authority as I already know who it is. "Where's your date?"

"Didn't bring one," I reply, looking over my shoulder to see my pack's future Alpha walking towards me. His dark green eyes lock with my own and I already know he's had a bad night. After all, his date is not beside him and his hair is all messed up from the last time I saw him. "What about yours?" I ask, looking back to the crowd as I can feel his eyes on the exposed skin of my back. Mother fell head over heels for this dress, showing it to me only for my heart to swell. I love this dress, a beautiful masterpiece of navy material, illusion sleeves with gems held in with the mesh that suits my skin color, the mermaid style beautiful as the end flares out just enough for easy maneuvering, and the back is open with crystals lining the material.

"She decided to leave my side a little early," Flynn mumbles, standing beside me as we look out upon the couples as a slow dance comes on.

I spot him. His blond hair stands out from his suit, his brown eyes locked on a certain individual as my heart feels a sharp sting. I want to cry. I hold myself calm and remind myself of what I have to do. Of how I have to put on a show. Watching, I notice how he looks at her, how he reaches out his hand for the girl so gently. The second she takes his hand, he pulls her in, twirling her around as I hear her beautiful laugh. It's beautiful, at least, that's how he described it the first time he told me about her. He told me about how her laugh and smile could make anyone fall head over heels for her. She holds his heart and he's certainly fine with that.

What does she have that I do not? She's got ginger hair that falls to her shoulders, tonight it's curled with her bangs braided back. She's got beautiful bright green eyes I would love to have, a tall yet thin body, and a gorgeous gold dress that is loose on her, yet she still pulls off the look. "Let me guess," Flynn begins, leaning back against the balcony as he faces me. "Trouble in paradise or did she backstab you?"

Meeting his eyes, I shake my head, looking back to the couple as he spins her around once more and they begin the slow dance. "She didn't do anything to me..." I trail off, my voice soft as Flynn leans in closer. "She did nothing."

He raises an eyebrow. "What did she do to him? You don't like her. You don't like her dating your best friend so what's up?"

A single tear rolls down my cheek, my hand flying up to brush it away as my wolf stirs within me. Arms wrap around my smaller frame, his body hard compared to mine as all I want is for him to hold me like this. For him to look at me the way he does to her. But it can never happen. No. Because we are best friends and he has always made that clear. I've tried. Three years I've know him, and for one year I've known who he is to me, yet I've seen him fall for someone who just randomly showed up one day. He fell head over heels for her and I had no control over it.

"I'm fine," I whisper, relaxing in Flynn's embrace as his dark green eyes meet mine once more.

He shakes his head. "You're a mess, Amory." I nod my head, knowing that Flynn is right and there's nothing I can do about it.

He knows. He knows my suffering because he's seen me lose my sanity and run off. "Anyone would be in your state."

"I just want to forget him. I just want to forget them together. I want to tell him, so damn bad I want to tell him..." I trail off. "But I can't because he's a damn human."

Flynn nods, resting his chin on my shoulder as I take one last look at the couple that people love to death. "He's my mate and I'm watching him fall in love with someone else."

"What are you going to do?" Flynn asks, his lips brushing my ear as I think of just leaving this town.

"I'm going to move away," I pause, "and never look back."

Chapter 2

I can recall years ago, exactly to the day I met him and we hit it off. He was outgoing and I was the typical shy girl finding her place in high school. For him, high school was a social experience where he made friends while he also learned. To him, I was the shy girl who some people knew and he wanted to know me, he wanted to make another friend. We become best friends, doing everything together from talking in the hall to having crazy experiences that we would laugh about for years to come. He was my muse. He broke the shell of the shy girl and devoted most of his time to me. But friends is all we ever could be. The night I turned seventeen and found that he was my mate, I was broken.

How do you tell your best friend that you love them more than a friend? It's hard. It's nerve racking…especially when you know they don't have eyes for you in that way.

I stand in the hallway, the school busy as chatter is all around me. Countless stores from prom night still are talked about, some of the couple's still together as they smile and laugh. One couple has caught my eye in particular, the couple that is breaking my heart and have no clue about it. What does Molly Moore have that I do not? She has my best friend and my one true mate, Augustus Brown.

I tear my eyes away as they walk down the hall, knowing that they will stop by me and have a small conversation. I know what will happen tonight for them. Augustus told me. He told me he was taking her to our favorite local restaurant. Grabbing the handle to my locker, I open it up and put a few books inside, wondering if I could just avoid them and leave for the day. Maybe I should. But if I cannot make it through this day then I cannot make it through the last two weeks of school. I have two weeks and then the summer begins. Once the summer is over, I plan on leaving and never looking back. I cannot live in a town where my mate is with someone else. Hell, I cried myself to sleep last night and prom night all because I cannot even reject my mate without him knowing I am not human.

I make my decision, heading for my next class and skipping the talk with Augustus and Molly. I have to get away from them at least. I cannot do that kind of torture and put on a happy face. Wearing masks will only hurt you at the end of the day more than you wish.

"You're going to have to face him sometime," I mutter to myself, passing Flynn and his future Beta, Cole, on the way to my first class. Even though Flynn's date dumped him two nights ago, he's already got a girl back by his side. She's werewolf, from our pack, and in the drama club here. I recall her being a sweetheart, but Flynn seems to bring out the worst in all of these girls. "Just think of the two weeks remaining and you'll be fine."

I enter my math class, taking a seat in the middle as no one is even in here. It's a ghost town and I have a good reason to be here, twenty minutes early. Molly is in this class as well, a straight A student with no teacher ever finding her a torture to teach. She's someone you cannot hate. She's someone, that although she has my mate, I could never hate her. Why? Because she has done nothing to me, hell, she only knows me as Augustus' best friend and nothing more. To her I'm just someone to get along with because she is dating my best friend for all she knows. She's with the man fate has paired me up with.

The minutes fly by and soon, after everyone has taken their seats, the room quiets down and a chair scratches across the floor. I already know who it is by their scent and the fact that we do this every Friday. "Run tomorrow morning before the sunrise? It will be fun," Flynn asks, putting his backpack down as he takes his seat beside me. "We've missed you lately."

I shrug. "Things have changed." He nods, knowing what I am referring to, how I don't like shifting that much. Every Tuesday morning a group of ten of us would meet up at four in the morning by the pack house and we run and watch the sunrise. The last time I took part in the event was four months ago. Four months ago when Augustus told me that he was in love with Molly.

"Your loss, Amory," he mutters just as the whiteboard is filled with Calculus and we spend the next hour taking notes. Every now and then Flynn will write something on my paper and have a small conversation. It mostly consists of school topics or pack business. You might be thinking why the future Alpha and I girl like me have conversations for, after all, the majority of werewolves at this school question it as well. It's as if there's some unspoken rule that if the future Alpha associates himself with an individual of the opposite sex, that they must have some tie to them. What's my tie to Flynn?

None. I simply joined his group of friends two years ago for early morning runs and we hit it off. I've seen him break up with countless girls, one in particular that caused him to knock on my window one night and just stay the night as he was heartbroken. She tossed him away the second she found someone else. She was a bitch and I agreed with him.

As the class ends and I leave the room as fast as possible, who awaits me the second I make it to the staircase causes my heart to skip a beat. Augustus stands there, hands in his pocket, his eyes upon me, and a smile on his face. "Amory!" I offer him a weak smile. "Where were you this morning?"

"I was late," I lie, not even taking the time for a pause to occur between the two of us. He simply raises an eyebrow and watches me as I look over my shoulder. I want to go for a run, I want to feel the wind in my hair and my paws hitting the ground. My wolf doesn't want to. She wants to be locked away. She's still mourning the loss of a mate. We know we have lost him. "I've got to get to my next class."

"You've never cared about being punctual," Augustus comments, stepping forward as his scent envelops me and my body instantly becomes warm. "Are you okay? Is there something wrong? Did I do something?"

Yes. He did something. He did something without even having the knowledge to know that he did it.

"I'm fine, nothing wrong," I say, my voice chirpy as I can hear Molly calling his name. "I'll leave the two of you." Stepping away, I scurry up the steps of the school, my legs feeling like jelly as I can hear them laughing down below. All I want is for Augustus to be by my side, for him to cuddle me, hold me, confess his feeling for me, and make me feel like I'm the only girl in the world day after day after day. But he cannot. He has someone else and he is in love with her.

"Amory!" I can hear him call out, the sound of his shoes against the pavement allowing me to know how far away he is. Simply, I take in a slow and deep breath, turning around to see Augusts chasing after me, worry in his eyes as my heart swells. At least I know that he cares for me, that he is drawn to me...but as a friend. As nothing more but a friend. It hurts me to realize. It hurts me to acknowledge. "You have some explaining to do. You're acting like we're in some fight."

I see Molly follow quickly behind him, her slender legs covered by a simple pair of jeans, her flat chest covered by a pretty white blouse. She's the girl that could wear a sun dress any day of the year and no one would question her, for they would not be able to take their eyes off her. She's not hot, not sexy, but she's beyond beautiful. She's the classy beautiful that lets you know she holds herself to high standards, has self control, and cares deeply for everyone. She doesn't get selfish. Augustus fell for her. He fell for the perfect girl, while his perfect match has been beside him for three years.

"Augustus, please, I'm tired right now and have a migraine," I inform, Augustus coming to a halt as he stands before me. Molly follows quickly behind, offering me a gentle smile as my wolf growls within me. I haven't heard from my wolf in hours. "I need to go."

"What's wrong, Amory?" Augustus asks. Pain fills my heart as I watch Molly take his hand, their fingers interlocking as all I can feel is pain. Pain. He causes me not only mental pain, but physical. Physical because I cannot reject him, because any moment I try and shift into my wolf, she digs herself deeper into a hole and I feel a pain within my chest.

"Nothing."

Unlocking my car, I leave them alone, driving off as my vision blurs. The waterworks occur as I drive, my hands shaking as sobs escape my mouth. Not wanting to go home, I pull over onto the side of the road, right to the entrance of the private drive to the pack house. I used to spend tons of time at the pack house until a year ago when I realized I had found my mate. Now, it is a distant memory, yet a warm one, one when I didn't feel pain every time I saw my mate. Back then I didn't have to watch my mate fall in love with someone else.

There's a knock on my car window. I jump, looking out to see a familiar face. Quickly I wipe away my tears, composing myself as I roll down the window and fake a smile. "Hey."

"Get into the passenger's seat, I'm taking you home, you're in no state to drive," he announces. Looking over my shoulder, I see his car parked behind mine, a girl looking pissed as she sits in there with no idea what to do.

"What about your date?" I ask. "I can drive myself back home."

Flynn, shakes his head. "Get in the passenger seat, Amory, I'm driving you home," he demands, his Alpha voice present as I know he's serious. Sighing, I climb over to the passenger seat, watching as Flynn hops into my Prius, rolling his eyes at the music playing. Turning off the music, he puts the car in drive and pulls out back onto the street. I look back around, seeing his date driving his car, his most prized possession as his parents spend a shitload on it. "You're in no state to be driving."

"Thanks, dad," I mutter, tone flooded with sarcasm as I look outside to see the trees pass by. "Thank you."

Flynn nods, meeting my gaze as I know he cares. He wants me to get home safe. He's doing what every Alpha should do: care for the pack members. Care for them even when they want to push the world away.

CHAPTER 3

The ride is silent, the radio softly playing as my shoulders are tense. The trees pass by quickly as my eyes glance to the side mirror, watching Flynn's date driving his car as she follows in pursuit. Looking back to the road, I recross my legs, the atmosphere tense as I just want to be alone, in the silence, my mind empty, and my heart no longer in pain. Flynn drives my car, his eyes locked on the road as he seems relaxed to me, his posture relaxed, hands on the wheel, and not in some horrible state like myself. To the world, he is free. He is not tied down to a world of emotions that eat you alive because your mate is with another. Has he found his mate? No. How do I know? When an Alpha finds his Luna, they cannot stop talking about her or even keep their eyes off of her, not to mention everyone would know by now. He has not found his mate, and I know he is growing impatient because everyone else is finding theirs.

"Do you plan on rejection?" Flynn asks, breaking the silence as my heart plummets to the floor. Those eyes flash through my mind and all I can focus on is a set of dreams. A set of dreams I've envisioned for months and months. Moments that wake me up at night, bringing me to tears as the rest of the night is filled with darkness and the sense of feeling as if I could never find another. Augustus is the perfect guy...the one my mother would love to see me being home and my father approve of. I've dreamt of us, of if we could be together. Moments of laughter and joy as we create a story to tell our children.

Augustus is the perfect guy.

But that doesn't mean he's the perfect match.

"No," I whisper, meeting Flynn's gaze as we pull up outside my house. As the engine shuts off, Flynn leans back in the seat, crossing his arms as my throat runs dry. "If I reject him he deserves the truth of what I am." He nods. "A human learning of our existence can be severely punishable, Flynn, and by rejecting Augustus I would be risking my life." Flynn nods once more, checking his phone as his car pulls up beside us. The window rolls down and his date for the night looks to us.

"Flynn, come on, let's go," she states, hopping out of the driver side as she walks around. She's impatient and I don't want to keep her waiting.

Sighing, I open my door, offering Flynn's date a gentle smile. "He's all yours." She rolls her eyes, yet offers me a smile in return. I like her. I like what I've seen, not because she's the best I've ever met, but because she hasn't cussed me out and claimed I was fucking her so-called boyfriend. She's pretty. She's like all the rest. With black hair that hits her shoulders in gentle curls, tan skin, slender and long legs, bright golden eyes, and a light sprinkle of freckles, she's exactly what Flynn would look for: able to turn heads. I've never talked with her before, but I know her name.

"Miranda," Flynn greets, opening the passenger door of his car for her. His eyes meet mine once more and he shuts the door, tossing me my keys. "Take care." I thank Flynn for the ride, heading up for the front door of my house. "Amory?" I turn around to see Flynn about to hop into his his. "Come for a run in the morning, let loose and relax."

I can't. "I'll try," I reply, knowing full well that I will be unable to. Unable to because I cannot shift. I cannot shift into my damn wolf because of some stupid broken heart. And how do you mend a broken heart? You move on. But how? How do you move on when there is not set standard on how to? Everyone mends their own differently and the only path I can see out of this is through forgetting. Through slowly pushing away the world and escaping. They warn you about running from your problems because they will only come to bit you in the ass. It's seen as karma. But what happens when our problems are picked upon in a society where tradition is? As a wolf, I am tied down to a pack and taught that the pack is my life, that I am part of a pack. But my problem exists within this pack, within this town. I have to run.

Run because once I'm out of here, my problems will be gone. Problem of being unable to be with or even reject my mate because he is human. Because I would risk my life, for if Augustus were to tell a soul, the Wolf King would come for me or my Alpha would make me rogue.

Opening up the front door, the smell of cooked food fills my lungs and I can hear my parents in the kitchen discussing the day. They are mates. More than that, they are high school sweethearts as well who have been in love for twenty-three years. My father came from this pack and my mother as well.

I skip the dinner, rather passing by the kitchen as I head down the hallway to my room. Putting my backpack upon the floor, I place myself upon the bed, running a hand through my hair.

He's beautiful. He's perfection. He's exactly what I've ever wanted, the very creation of my dreams.

He watches me, not feeling a thing different as we make eye contact. After all, to him, this day is simply my birthday and not the day that I've noticed him as my mate.

"Amory, you okay?" One of my friends asks, pulling my attention off of my mate as my wolf wants to be let loose and run after him. Nodding, I walk through the crowd of school, heading after him as I pick up his scent.

Hallway after hallway I follow his scent, on cloud nine as I spot him, leaning against his locker as he shoves a book into his bag. Making my way over to him, I stop in my steps, my eyes following his own.

He's in a trance, those beautiful eyes not looking at me, but following a beautiful ginger as she crosses the hallway. He watches her with hope and deep interest.

He looks at her the way I look at him.

He looks at her as if she...is his.

Tears flow down my cheeks, a hand covering my mouth as I let out a sob. The day I discovered he was my mate I watched him look at another. That day I lost myself.

I lost my identity and my heart.

I'm running out of time.

I'm running out of fucking time because he is supposed to be mine. He is supposed to be my forever yet to me, he is my greatest poison. I'm like Socrates. He's my hemlock and I've taken a drink.

I've submerged my life into a world where all I can wonder if he notices me, if he will ever look at me the way that he looks at her. I've poisoned myself with love and have found myself slowly falling into an endless abyss.

I have to tell myself everyday that it's okay, that one day it will all get better and maybe, just maybe Augustus will be mine one day. That one day the Moon Goddess will understand the pain I have suffered and reward me in the end...but this is what a blind person would say.

My phone rings.

Checking the ID, my stomach twists into knots and my skin pales.

"Hey."

He's silent for a few seconds. "I miss you, Amory." My heart clenches. I wished he missed me in the way that I wanted him to. "I know you have to be going through something...I don't know what, but I know you're hurting."

He has no idea he is the cause of this and his words are just a catalyst to my suffering.

"Augustus..." I trial off, wiping away a tear. "I-

"Augustus." My heart skips a beat as I hear her call out his name. She's with him. Of course she is. He's in love with her, he's told me. He's told me more than once.

"Amory, I've got to go, I have to drive Molly home."

I hold on a sob. "I understand."

The line goes silent, the phone falling from my hand as I finally let out a sob.

Do I really understand? Understand that he can never be mine? That the man fate made to be perfect for me...is not mine. And he never could be.

CHAPTER 4

The end of the week could not come faster. With my final transcripts to be sent out to my college in a week and finals starting in three days, I know my days are counting down. As for the rest of my senior class, they are more than happy to get out of high school, ready just as I am to break free and never look back. But they have different motives for why they plan on never looking back. Their's are because a future awaits them of excitement and living in the past of high school can only weigh one down. As for me, I need to break free from here because the chains around my feet burn through my skin every second. I cannot look back because it reminds me one of the toughest moments I've ever experienced and am still suffering through: my mate falling in love with someone. Someone other than me.

Molly strolls through the classroom, taking a seat next to me as I question her. She's never sat next to me in Econ and quite frankly, I'm not her biggest fan. Sure, Molly is impossible to hate, but she has hurt me with no idea. "Hey," she greets, offering me a joyful smile as I examine her for the day. Her ginger hair is curled with her bangs braided back, her attire consists of a blush pink blouse and jean shorts, and her overall persona for the day is joyful. I've never seen this girl cry nor yell. I've never seen her suffer like I have, never face rejection, never feel mental pain. She's always strong, she's perfect. She's the perfect girl for someone, but she can't be for Augustus. Augustus is my perfect match and boy, yet he is not mine. At least not now. Not yet. Maybe one day he will come around, maybe one day he won't introduce me as his best friend...but his girlfriend, or even wife. Maybe one day. Maybe one day the sun will come out and shine light in my life as my patience and pain is paid off.

But fate is a tricky individual. A tricky idea.

"So I was wondering if you'd like to come to a party tonight. Augustus was going to ask you, but he couldn't find you at lunch so I volunteered." I hate it. I hate how she is all his and I cannot do a thing about it. I hate that ai cannot hate this girl who is falling in love with the man I am supposed to have. I hate how he holds her and kisses her, I am jealous of their every second together. I am jealous that she gets all of him and I have nothing but a friendship. "He really wants you to come you know," she comments, causing me to raise an eyebrow. "Augustus says you've been distant and he misses you at parties."

I stopped going because she was always by his side, always holding his hand as people commenting on how cute of a couple they are.

"Please do it for him. He really misses you hanging out." He misses me. He does miss me...but he doesn't realize that he misses me because we are perfect for each other. "Do it for him."

He wants me there. He is my mate and he wants me around him, even if he doesn't understand that we are meant to be. This means that the mate bond is not just a fictional aspect, but there is a pull. But he thinks he misses me because we are best friends, not because we are perfect together.

"I'll try," I reply, looking back to the teacher as class starts up and I'm left alone to my thoughts. After a quiz and final remarks from the teacher, I pack up quickly, dreading to run into Molly once more as I rush out of the room. As I head down the hallway and take two left turns to avoid running into Augustus, I run into a sight I'm not too found of seeing: Flynn and another male in a fight. They other is human, getting a pounding as Flynn lands another punch right into the boy's jaw.

"What the hell!" I shout, running over just as Flynn is about to punch the poor guy again. This one is human, meaning Flynn could easily kill him. We have rules within our pack, ones about fighting humans, how we should never use our full power upon them or we will get in massive trouble. "Let him go," I snap, grabbing Flynn's arm just as he recoils it.

The human's eyes widen, his nose bloody and his eyebrow cut as well. He looks like a mess unlike Flynn, whose only sign of blood comes from his knuckles due to the human. He's mad. The future Alpha is mad, but why? What did this human do or say to push his buttons? "What the hell is wrong with you," I snap, lightly slapping the Alpha to keep his wolf from surfacing and put his attention on me.

Flynn tries to control his breathing as I look to the human, a junior that's part of band. I've talked to him once during a fire drill but I don't recall his name. Whatever he did to Flynn must of been bad. "Move along," I order, watching as he nods his head, running off as I turn back to the angry alpha male. "What's wrong with you!? He's merely a human!"

Flynn rolls his eyes, grabbing his backpack as he heads for the boy's locker room. He thinks he can just get out of this. I know full well that no one is in the locker room, so I follow Flynn, watching as he pulls off his hoodie and places his backpack down on a bench. "What did the human do?" Those dark green eyes meet my own and I'm warned off. The hairs on the back of my neck stand up and I watch as Flynn washes off his knuckles, releasing a deep breath as I lean against a cold locker.

"It's not business to concern yourself with," he mumbles, avoiding eye contact now as he grabs his navy hoodie, pulling it back over his gray shirt as I get a peek at the abs hidden under that shirt. "Just go to class, Amory."

"Flynn, you could of seriously hurt yourself. You hardly get into fights and knowing that piece of information I know it has to of been-"

"Why?! Why the hell do you concern yourself with conflicts that you are not part of, Amory?!" Flynn growls, the lockers shaking as my skin pales. "You have no play in my life so why do you care?!"

Why is he doing this? Why is he speaking to me like this when yesterday he helped me our? Why is he talking to me like this when I've helped him out multiple times?

"Why do you care so much about me?" He asks, his voice demanding as his wolf begins to surface. My eyes well up with tears, my stomach turning into a mess of knots as my throat drys. "Tell me, Amory, why do you give a damn?"

Using the back of my hand, I wipe away a tear, backing up to the door of the locker room.

"Maybe because my mate and best friend is falling in love with someone else as I sit back and watch. Maybe because no one but you has comforted me in this time. Maybe because you're one of my only friends!" I cry, opening up the door as I look over my shoulder to Flynn. "Maybe because I thought you cared about me and we were friends. Friends care for one another and I thought I was repaying the help you've given me, so excuse me for trying to be a friend," I snap, slamming the or behind me as the hallway is empty before me.

By the end of the day I'm laying down upon my bed, my head spinning with questions about the upcoming month or so. Mom and dad went out for the night on a date, telling me dinner was in the fridge and telling me that they loved me. Love. What even is love? Will I even get a chance to ever experience it because it looks like I can't even get my mate to simply think about me as more than a friend. There's a party tonight, one that Augustus wants me to attend. He misses me and this party is a chance to show him that I care, to show him that he not only wants, but also needs my company. But Augustus is in love. My mate is in love with someone other than me.

Hell, everyone is going against me. I thought Flynn was a friend, I thought he cared for my wellbeing...but when I tried to aid him he pushed me away. He pushed me away just as everyone does.

Getting up, my feet turn cold against the wooden floor and I make my way to my closet. Pulling open the door, I search for an outfit for the night, knowing it will be a party filled with drinking, smoking, games, and heartbreak. I've come to accept heartbreak every awakening moment of my days that I am still tied down to this town. As I pull on a pair of jean shorts and a navy blouse, I'm set up already for failure tonight as I slide on my shoes and pull my hair up in a bun. I'm ready to get my heart broken tonight, but I'm already to show Augustus that needs me around. That we need one another. But how? How can I do that when Molly is by his side and he loves her. How do you make someone fall out of love without feeling like the biggest jerk to ever walk the earth? I have no idea how, but I know fate has placed us together.

Grabbing my keys from the kitchen counter, I head out the house, hopping into my car as I read my head back on the seat. Tonight I have no idea what to expect except for seeing Molly and Augustus look at each other as if they are mates. As my headlights are switched on and I pull out of the driveway, my eyes are locked on the road, the darkness of the night surrounding me as I plug in the address. I have two tasks tonight: to not run into Flynn and to show Augustus that he needs me to live. Maybe my goals in life should be higher, but for now, they are all that matter to me.

I need to push Flynn's rejection as a friend from my mind and focus on Augustus, because he is who I am to love. He is my perfect match, even if he doesn't see it.

Chapter 5

"Didn't expect to see you here," he comments, causing me to jump out of my skin. I didn't think to see him here so soon, or maybe because he anticipated me as a mate should. As I turn around, a smile spreads across his face as I can feel my wolf pawing to be let out and claim him as ours. "You finally came out of that shell of yours." Augustus hands me a drink, looking back to the crowd doing a game of dares including shots. "I haven't talked to you for what seems like weeks."

He misses me.

"I've been busy. College and all," I remark, wth as Augustus runs a hand through his blond hair, eyes eyes scanning my face. He feels it! He has to feel it, the mate bond, how he is drawn to me. My heartbeat increases, watching as he simply places a hand on my shoulder, sparks flying through my skin. He has to feel this! He has to feel the sparks!

"Have you seen Molly? She should be here by now?" The smile once upon my face falls down into a faint frown, the sparks feeling full now as Molly clouds my once happy thoughts. "I'm glad she talked you into coming tonight." Anger. I want to unleash my wolf and claw that human into shreds and claim this man as my own. The need to find that human and tell her to back off, to tell her to never look back and leave Augustus to me...that need is building up inside of me and it frightens me. I have nothing against her other than my mate is helplessly in love with her and there's not a damn thing I can do about it. The only thing she has done is have Augustus fall in love with her...she's never hurt me purposefully nor do I think she ever could. I can't hate her. Damnit I can't hate her because Augustus loves her, and that means I have to be kind to her. Because my mate loves her I have to respect that. Why? Because I love him.

Augustus walks off, leaving me behind as he searches the party for the redhead. Taking a swing of the beer he handed me, I head off to find my own muse for the night. I got here and it would be a waste of time to just leave now. Before Augustus fell for Molly, parties were a massive part of my life. Augustus and I were teammates for beer pong, we lost and and we won some as I remember feeling alive as he would pull me in for a tight hug if we won a game. It used to be fun going to these events, how I would partake in the dare games or even dance away with some friends from other classes. But it all changed when I saw him watched her the day I discovered who he truly was to me. My life flipped upside down and I pushed many people away without an explanation. How would you feel if the man you knew you were destined to be with loved another? If you had to smile and support them because you knew he was happy? It feels like a never ending war within you to either tell him how you feel and claim him...or sit back and watch as he writers another chapter of his life with you just in the background.

"Someone looks like they've had a rough day," someone states from beside me. Looking to the individual, I raise an eyebrow at them, wanting to know what they're up it. "I mean, no one has to get to know you to see that you're looking miserable." Gavin Knox stands beside me, leaning against the doorframe to the dinning room, his gray eyes locked on mine. He's what you would think of as your stereotypical 'bad boy' based on the usual attire of a leather jacket and bruised knuckles from a fight, but after knowing him for seven years, you see he's quite the mommy's boy. Sure, he likes the daily fights and enjoys getting into trouble, but outside of school he doesn't dare disrespect his parents or pack.

"Since when are you licensed to get into others business and state things that are not true," I mumble, taking another swing of the beer as I find Molly, her back to me, chatting with an old friend of hers. "Everyone has their ups and downs, Gavin, and some choose to keep them secret."

He chuckles, taking out his phone as the light illuminates his face for a quick second. Locking the device, he slides it back into his pocket, meeting my stare as a smirk forms across his face. We used to be running partners Freshmen year solely because we shifted into our wolves for the first time two weeks apart. We learned about our wolf forms together and became good friends. He's one of the friends I pushed away months ago. "You look like shit, Amory, let's get down to the basics here. I know you're little secret just as Flynn does. A few of us are not too blind to see the fact that you're heartbroken."

"You have no idea what I'm going through," I snap, my wolf wanting to surface.

"And how could that be? I've faced heartb-

"You're mate isn't in love with someone else, Gavin, now is she?" I snap, looking pack his shoulder to see his mate, Hellen, laughing at some joke as she looks beautiful. Hellen is my cousin and Gavin's mate, both accepting one another a year ago. "You never watched Hellen fall in love with someone else and have no idea that you were more to her than just a friend, now did you?"

Gavin shuts his mouth, knowing anything he says, he can really have no insight in because he's never experienced it. He's never experienced what the hell I'm facing right now and have been for months. Looking to Hellen, I watch as she waves at me, one of the few females she trusts around her man. We grew up together for the most part, my mom and her dad siblings. Gavin nods his head, heading back into the room as he leaves me behind. I know I'm pushing people away, but when all they try and say is stuff that deals with what I'm going through, I shut off my ears. They don't have any experience in my situation and I hope they never do.

"Amory." I know that voice. "Hey, Augustus was looking for you, we want to know if you'd be up for some dare games," Molly asks, a smile across her face as I know I cannot turn her down, especially when Augustus wants me there. She loves him, I can see it, I can hear it. The way she talks about him and looks at him. He has her and she has him. I don't have either.

We head to the second floor of the house, into a storage room as seven other seniors are in a circle, a bottle of tequila and two shot glasses in the center. Already my wolf is unsure of what is to come tonight, knowing that these games can get pretty intense. Taking my seat, Augustus smiles at me, causing my heart to swell and my wolf to jump with glee. The rules are stated, that you either take the dare or you take two shots. Simple to understand, but you also have to know your alcohol limit. It's harder than it looks, because you have to understand that if you take the shots early on and aren't in the right state of mind in the later rounds, who knows what kind of dare you'll agree to. Know your limits. It's more like chess than checkers. To win? Don't fuck up. You fail a dare and you are thrown into the pool outback.

"Let's start," one of the guys states, staring off the challenge with a spin of the bottle. Whoever the bottle lands on, they do the dare, then they spin the bottle and pick the dare for the next and so forth.

After the third round, I've done minor dares such as switching the music downstairs to tasteless music, smashing a beer bottle on a jock's head (who thankfully was a wolf), and was thankfully missed the third round. With no alcohol in me except for the beer, I've watched one human girl already take four shots and turn down a dare, two of the guys carrying her out and throwing her into the pool. With one down we play again.

By the time I'm watching one of the girls spin the bottle for her victim, my eyes meet Augustus's stare. He's been watching me ever since he took his first two shots in the fourth round. As the bottle keeps spinning and spinning, our eyes never leave one another's, as if locked in some trance. It's the mate bond. I know it is.

The bottle lands on Augustus. He'll take the dare. He's competitive when he's had a short or two. "Augustus," the girl, who I have believe is called Maddie, announces, a small smirk crossing her face. She's up to something. Looking my way, she offers me a sly smile, opening her mouth to tell the dare. "Make out with Amory."

A few guys hoot in the room as my skin is drained of all of its pigment. I watch as Augustus's eyes widen and Molly, Molly a bit tipsy from her three rounds of shots as she doesn't think much of the dare.

"Do the dare or take the shots. You can't fail this one and be ejected from the game," Maddie informs. But Augustus understands the risks of another two shots. Another two shots and he'll be far gone for sure. He's human and has a weak stomach.

I watch as he slides over, my eyes wide as he takes in a deep breath. "Just a dare," he mumbles, making himself certain as my heart falls a bit. This is just a dare and he's tipsy. I'm just a dare and a drunk mistake. I'm just part of the game.

His lips meet mine and sparks fly through my body, my skin on fire as I feel like I'm on cloud nine. Touchdown! It's all I want. It's all I want to remember. I want to always remember that I kissed my mate, even if it's not a true kiss. Even if there's no passion, desire, or even care involved. As Maddie calls that the time is up, Augustus pulls away and everything seems to slow down. I know he felt it. He felt the sparks and the ignition within his heart. But when he thinks about it, he will only remember it as a drunk dare.

As Augustus takes back his seat and spins the bottle, I look to Molly. Her eyes are on him, a firm line on her face. They will be good in the morning when their heads are cleared up. She's forgive him because she knows he loves her and it was just a dare. That it meant nothing. But it will never feel like nothing.

As the rounds pass and four more people are ejected from the game, I decide to end my turn. I let myself become checkmate as

I'm thrown into the water and quickly resurface. I need to clear my mind for the rest of thought. I need to be free and forget the night. I didn't take a single shot, I didn't fail a dare either. I wanted to end the game.

As I head to my car, my phone buzzes. As I hope into my car and start up the engine, it buzzed again. Looking down I see the message from Augustus that shatters my heart.

It was a dare. It can't happen again. I know it was a dare and you know we are best friends, but it can't happen again.

I drive.

Chapter 6

She watches me closely, taking in every small movement I make as she sits in the back. How her eyes are locked on me let's me know that something is off, that the small conversations we had will soon change, and that she sees me differently now. No longer does she think of me as her boyfriend's best friend, but now as someone to be cautious of. Ever since Friday night, ever since a week ago, all she has done is watched and be like a predator observing their prey before the kill. Little does Molly know that in this jungle called high school, I am one of the predators that lurks and waits. I am a predator, I'm a predator of the moon that is still hunted down. Years and years ago hunts would take place after my kind, myths were formed, and horror stories were told.

I am a predator. She is not. I am the predator that is watching my prey slowly lead my mate to her. However, I've watched as my mate falls endlessly in love with her. The last thing I want is drama, but I want my mate. I want to stop suffering. I don't want to feel weak and pathetic. I can't just go and tell Augustus. I can't go up to him, reject him, and give him no explanation for what I mean or the heartbreak he will undergo. When rejection occurs, only pain will follow, it's something I will have to accept if I do reject him.

As the bell rings, I rush out of class, holding my head high as I know in two days I will receive my diploma and be free. Within three months I will be in college, two states away, in Florida, and starting a new chapter in my life. Maybe with Augustus being rejected, or maybe with him still holding my heart as he simply doesn't notice it. That text he sent me, he was nervous, he was scared. Scared why? Scared because he felt something. He felt those spark some, the feeling of his heart speeding up, the mate bond that brings mates together. He's scared because he didn't regret kissing me, and because of that, he's afraid that his relationship with Molly is threatened. Even she sees it.

She sees me as an opponent now. Maybe she will put it behind her, but she's mad. She's mate because Augustus and I shared one kiss.

Once out of the school building, my heart only drops to my feet as I spot Flynn. I haven't chatted with him since he told me off, he told me to forget about it and left. I thought he was a friend. I thought he could help me in my darkest moments. He's not with a girl, nor a friend, or anyone, but he's by my car, his parked beside mine as he sits on the hood of his, those eyes locked on mine. My wolf feels submissive already as our future Alpha watches us like a hawk. I am more afraid of Flynn than Molly. I don't think he would ever hurt me, but I know he holds authority over me and Molly only holds jealousy.

"Amory," Flynn greets, watching as I unlock my car and put my backpack in the back seat. "How are you last days in school coming along?" Small chat that will soon end and a conversation will begin. "Happy you'll be out soon, overjoyed? Relieved?"

Slamming the back door shut, I turn to Flynn, my jaw clenched. "Happy," I mumble, crossing my arms as Flynn quickly glances back to the school and then to me. "What's the purpose of this conversation, Flynn, there has to be some catch?"

"A catch?" He asks, a lopsided smile gracing his face as I lean against my car.

"Please, Flynn, the last time we talked you practically kicked me out and told me we were not even friends."

"It's hard to explain-"

"I need a friend, Flynn, one who doesn't pity me every moment of my life. I need a friend who will make me smile, not cry. You were that friend," I snap, Flynn's eyebrows furrowing together as I tell the future alpha off. He's not happy with how I'm talking to him, but he understands.

"Friends?" He begins, shaking his head. "Friends do look out for one another and aid the other in their darkest moments, but friends have a connection." I await his next words. "We have no connection."

Dick.

I land one strong punch to his face, hearing the cracking of bone as I do so. Flynn is thrown off of his car by the force, landing upon the ground as attention is drawn to us. "Go to hell," I snap, hopping into my car as the future alpha gets up from the ground, glaring at me as I drive off. I've just disrespect the future Alpha...that means I've just signed myself up for a living hell. Flynn gets up, charging at my car as my wolf feels submissive. I should of never have done that.

I drive, my tires screeching as Flynn only holds a cold glare at me. My phone rings, the familiar ringtone echoing throughout the vehicle as my throat runs dry. He's mad. He has a reason to be. Declining, the call, I take a sharp left turn, knowing better than to head back home. Just as silence fills the car once again, the ringtone starts up again, this time a different ringtone sounding.

"Augustus," I greet, knowing that this conversation will be difficult to commit to. "What's up?" I ask, coming to a stop as I'm parked before a small look out of the town.

"Can you come over, Amory, please?" Augustus asks, practically begging for me to come over. I don't think on it, knowing that my mate is in need of something rather important. I have to be there for my mate, even if they are not mine. Yet. Taking my car back, I find myself driving through the familiar streets of town, already knowing the directions inside and out.

"What's wrong?" I ask, taking another right turn as the familiar houses line the street. "School? Family?"

"Molly."

Relationship troubles. I'm screwed.

"I'll be there soon." Hanging up, I drive for ten more minutes, soon arriving at the house of Augustus and his family. A picture of perfection with the suburb house, two stories, tall windows, a SUV out front, Camaro, and truck in the driveway, and a white picket fence. Augustus's family has always been seen as perfection, the doctor husband and nurse wife, a dog, and a son who has big plans in the future. But it wasn't that that made Augustus perfect in my eyes. His smile was the first thing to draw me in before we were mates, his kindness, his caring features, his humor, and so much more.

Getting out of the car, I head for the front door, knocking twice as I wait patiently. As the door opens, Augustus stands before me, his hair a mess of blond locks, bags under his eyes, and his clothes winkled. "What's going on? You look like shit?"

Augustus laughs shortly. "I could say the same for you," he comments, motioning to my dark bags and unbrushed hair all pulled back in a bun. We both look like shit. I don't know why he does and he has no idea why I do. "Come in."

I follow Augustus up the familiar wooden stairs, his dog greeting me as usual as we walk down the hall. As he opens the white door to his room, I can smell her. Molly is all over his room, her scent everywhere from her being here too often. It's as if the room reeks of her.

With the door shut behind us, I watch as Augustus takes a seat at the foot of his bed, raising an eyebrow as I lean against the dark green walls. "What's up with you lately?" He asks. "You're not a stranger, come here." I usually would sit beside him, cracking a joke or showing me something from the day on his phone.

"I'm fine here."

He tilts his head, confused at my actions as I rather move to his desk, sitting at the chair there. "What did you call me about? What's up with Molly?"

Augustus shakes his head, letting out a deep breath as he grabs his phone. Running his fingers along the screen, he looks up to me under his eyelashes. "She's...we've had a small fight and are on a break." My wolf perks up, telling me to take advantage of this moment, to show him my true feeling and claim him as ours. But that is wrong. He's in a time of need, a time of need for a friend. He needed and friend and that is why I am here. I am the friend he called and by making a move upon him, that would be manipulating him.

"What went wrong?" I ask, crossing my arms as Augustus shrugs his shoulders.

"She's been talking about you." My eyes widen. "About how we are together too much and it doesn't seem like I'm fully involved in our relationship." Augustus gets up from the bed, placing his phone done.

"It's because of that party," I explain, my posture becoming stuff as Augustus stands a foot away from me. "She should know I oppose no threat to your relationship."

Augustus slides his hands into his pockets, nodding as he looks down at me with those eyes. Goddess those eyes that reel me in and make me want to claim him as mine. I want Molly out of the picture.

"Give her time," I add. "Give Molly some time, maybe send we flowers one day. She will come back." I cannot allow my mate to become miserable. I cannot manipulate my mate. "She will put it behind her and so will you."

Getting to my feet, I'm about to head for the door, only for Augustus to stop me. "Did that kiss mean nothing to you?"

He has me in checkmate. I cannot lie to him yet I cannot watch him become manipulated and risk a relationship that makes him happy. "What does that have to do with anything?" I question, turning around to face Augustus.

"Answer the question, Amory, or I will come to a conclusion. What did the kiss mean to you? Did it mean nothing?"

My throat becomes dry and my mouth does as well, my palms becoming sweaty as I know I cannot lie. I cannot lie to Augustus.

"You want to know the entire truth?" He nods. I run a stressful hand through my hair. "The truth, Augustus.....it's...." I lose my words, my body becoming overheated as my mind runs through thousands of possibilities. "The truth is that it was just a dare. It was part of a game and you played the game. You took the dare and I understand."

Augustus nods, his eyes showing sadness as I head back for the door. Pulling it open, he doesn't say another word. I run from the room almost, quickly walking down the stairs as I head right for the front door. Just as I reach the front porch as my Prius comes to view, I hear him come after me.

"Amory," he calls out, my head turning as I look over my shoulders. "I know that's a lie."

He's right, it was a lie, but I could not take advantage of his state of mind if I told him the truth. I could not risk taking advantage of my mate, I could not make Augustus suffer.

"If that's what you believe," I respond.

"Would you ever lie to me, Amory?" Augustus asks, concern in his eyes as I unlock my car.

I don't answer, rather hoping into my car and driving away. All I ever do is run from my problems. I never have the guts to face them. I never do.

CHAPTER 7

With my hair pulled back, headphones in my ears, playlist going, and my body sweaty, I make my way around the next block. My legs begin to bun slightly, my human form all I can work on now as my wolf refuses to shift for me. Instead of the usual morning run in wolf form through the woods, I've decided to stick to jogging every morning five miles or even more still satisfied. With a song that gets my blood pumping, I pick up speed, making sure to not take a familiar street as I know what lies down there. Who? Flynn, the future Alpha and classmate I punched yesterday.

With my body sweaty and my thirst for water present, I push forward, remembering my chat with Augustus last night. How he asked me about this kiss, how I lied, how he knew I had lied. I focus on his words, pushing myself on and on as I try and zone out of yesterday's events.

Just as I turn down the next street, I pick up the sound of a car approaching, the wheels crushing the gravel under it, the music soft. I know who it is. Pushing forward, I ignore the individual, holding a poker face as they call out my name. "Amory," he calls out again, pulling up beside me as he parks his car, hopping out of the vehicle. Running after me, he grabs my shoulder, causing me to lose all control over my poker face as I look his way and acknowledge him. "What the hell?"

"What do you want, Flynn?" I ask, my tone stern as I stop jogging and stand still, arms crossed. "I'm trying to jog here without–

I'm cut off with his eyes turning black. He's not happy with me whatsoever. The future alpha is pissed and I have an idea that it has to deal with the black bruising upon his nose. "Amory, what is going on with you?" I tilt my head, motioning for him to carry on with whatever point he is trying to make. "I've never seen you run in your life unless in training. You haven't run with us in wolf form for months. Why aren't you shifting?"

I can't let him know. I cannot let him know the truth. I cannot just unleash the truth that Augustus's relationship with someone has driven my wolf to the point of no return. Sure, she's still with me, still present, but she will not shift. I cannot just unleash a truth like that, not because of in scared of being seen a weak or pathetic, but because Flynn will try and take matters into his own hands. Any Alpha who knows a pack member is suffering feels like they have to take matters into their own hands. Flynn should not be involved in my mate bond with a human. A human who knows that the kiss we shared meant more to me. I wasted my chance to express my feeling for him, yet I lied. I ruined my only chance, but Augustus is suffering. He is in love with a girl who has put him through a rocky time, meaning that he is easy to take advantage of at the moment. If his best friend confesses their love for him, plus a mate bond is present, that means I am taking advantage of him. I tell Augustus when I feel like it's free will, when I come to terms that I cannot suffer anymore and tell him.

"Amory? Just tell me," Flynn snaps, grabbing my arm as he pulls me over to his car. "Either tell me the easy way or hop in the car and we do it the hard way."

"You have no business being involved in what's going on with me," I growl, shoving at the future Alpha. His eyes become black and the hairs stand up on the back of my neck.

"Get in the damn car."

I follow, hopping into the passenger seat as the luxury leather surrounds me. Flynn is soon to get in, turning down the volume as he takes ahold of the steering wheel. Turning off my music, I face the future Alpha, wanting to just exit the car and not let him know something that is eating me alive.

"Now, why haven't you shifted in months? Not only am I worried, but your parents have approached my mother on the topic." If my parents approached the Luna, then that means I have got explaining to do. But how do I tell my parents that I haven't shifted because my mate is my best friend and head over heels for Molly. Or at least is sort of head over heels for her. "Is it because of Augustus?"

He's got me. He doesn't even need an explanation. He already knows the cause of my suffering. "So you haven't shifted because of Augustus? Your wolf is too depressed to shift?"

"And stubborn," I mutter, at least adding in my two cents.

Flynn takes in a deep breath, stepping on the gas as I already know where he's trying to take me. The more we are surrounded by trees, the more I become restless. Tree after tree I know what Flynn has planned. As the car soon begins to slow, my jaw clenches as the familiar forest floor lays before us, the scent of pine strong, the memories present. I used to spend much of my free time in this part of the forest, where I first learned to hunt in wolf form, where my mother would take me to run, to teach me different tricks. Happy memories are only found here, ones of laughter and good times, where my family would be for the weekend, a small waterfall five miles in.

"Get out," Flynn orders, his wolf's tone present and I know better than to upset a future Alpha.

Hopping out of the car, my legs carry me to the tree line, Flynn locking the car as he places his keys behind one of the rims on a tire. Turning to me, he nods, motioning for me to shift.

"Flynn–

"Shift," he orders, his canines beginning to show as my eyes widen.

"I-I can't," I barely even state, my voice weak as Flynn shakes his head.

"Not on my damn watch. You are shifting today."

Flynn grabs my elbow, pulling me into the woods as I know he wants me to shift. He wants me to experience that freedom again. Shifting is not just a gift from the moon goddess, but it's a chance to feel free, to break free from the human realm and experience a world with no chains. In wolf form different senses are present, new places reachable, and new sensations. Imagine the moist forest floor after a light rain, the forest damp, the clouds filling the sky in a light gray shade, your paws digging through the soft ground, the wind in your fur. All of these sensations are what makes you look forward to shifting.

Flynn stops in the center of a tiny clearing, the sun behind a few clouds, the birds chirping in the woods. "I need you to concentrate, Amory, to concentrate on your bones snapping-

"Not the most present thought you know," I comment, a small smile breaking upon my face as Flynn crosses his arms.

"Try and connect with her."

I can't. She's dug herself a hole deep down in myself to where I cannot reach her. Whenever I try and reach for her, she only goes back to her hiding place. She escapes back to Mordor where I cannot reach her because I'm all the way on Galafray.

"Concentrate, Amory."

I shut my eyes, taking in a deep breath as I focus on the pattern of my breathing and the pumping of my blood through my veins. With my heartbeat calming down, my mind running black, I try and find her, trying to dig deeper and deeper to find her. I've barely even scratched the surface and already she's digging herself deeper. My mind turns fuzzy and my head begins to spin. She doesn't want to be found.

"Amor-

"I can't!" I scream, my eyes shooting open as I see Flynn before me, his eyes centimeters away from my own. "I can't shift into her because she doesn't want to shift. You know how no consent means rape, well she doesn't give me her consent."

Flynn let's out a deep breath.

"Why do you care?"

"What?" Flynn asks, raising an eyebrow as I feel myself frustrated.

"Why do you care if I can shift or not!? It makes no difference to you so why do you care?" I ask, shoving the future Alpha away as I want my answers now.

He doesn't reply, only letting the silence fill the air.

"Why?"

"Amory-

"Why? Why do you care about just some pack member?" I demand, my eyebrows furrowing together. Just as I'm about to turn and head back to the car, I'm pulled forward, my eyes widening as Flynn holds me close, his lips barely even an inch from my own.

"Because, Amory, you're not just some pack member."

CHAPTER 8

"Listen to me, Amory," Flynn calls out, running after me as I push open the front doors. "Amory!" Heads turn towards me, eyes locked upon the scene before them as either, from the viewer, their future alpha runs after a heartbroken pack member, or the 'bad boy' of the school runs after the best friend of Augustus.

As I reach the parking lot, I know he's gaining on me. Hell, he even parked two cars down from me unlike across the whole parking lot. Yesterday he said those words that sent me running home, on my own two feet and not looking back. Flynn didn't come after me, knowing rather to respect my personal space than intrude. How can this even be happening? How can he just say something like that to a girl who has found her mate and he has a mate somewhere out there? Hell, he should of found his mate two years ago when most of his title do. He should know that his mate awaits him, somewhere out there in this world that is tainted by sin.

"Amory, just listen to me," Flynn explains, grabbing my arm as I approach my little, blue Prius. I remember the first time I drove it here, Augustus made fun of it in a friendly manor, a smile gracing my face as I playfully punched his shoulder. Now this car is my escape from the world. All I do is drive away. "Just listen."

"You have a mate out there, Flynn," I snap, looking to the future Alpha, those green eyes meeting mine. "You know I have found my mate. You cannot just go saying these words to me. You cannot just say these phrases when I'm in a rough patch in my life."

"A mate that doesn't even know what he means to you," Flynn argues, grabbing ahold of my shoulders as he presses me lightly against my car. "Augustus does not see you as anything more than a friend and you still go for it. I don't have a mate, I don't think I'll ever get one, and here you are, the girl that has me head over heels for you like some cliché dumb blond movie."

I know Flynn is wrong. I know he is. Augustus, the words he spoke to me, how he did feel something. That kiss meant something to Augustus and I know that because of that, there is hope for me. Hope that the moon goddess may finally be answering my prayers.

"You're wrong," I snap, shoving at Flynn, seeing from the corner of my eyes Augustus waking out from the school. The last thing I want is for him to interfere here. Not because he is my mate, but because he is my best friend, and he knows he will do whatever it takes to protect me. Maybe there's a mate bond too that includes that, but Augustus has always seen me as his best friend. Sure, now he is beginning to feel things, but I know that in the end, he will chose Molly because he loves her more. But I have a mate. Flynn still has his to find and I cannot come in his way of that. "You have a mate and once you find her, you will know that what I saw is only helping you."

"What you're doing is denying both of us of a beautiful relation-ship."

There he goes. He just took out the big guns by saying relation-ship. He dropped the bomb and I know he's will stay fixated upon that thought. "We hardly know anything about-

"Hey! Flynn, what's going on?"

I'm screwed.

Augustus is speed-walking over, his eyes fixed upon the two of us. Already I know it's the mate bond. He's protective and jealous. This whole day is only going to get worse now. "What's going on, Flynn?" Augustus demands, shoving the future Alpha. Released from Flynn's grasp, my eyes widen as Augustus takes ahold of Flynn's leather jacket, pulling him close for intimidation. "Amory, are you okay?" Augustus asks, looking over his shoulder to me as I can hear Moly calling out his name. This is where it gets even messier.

"I'm good," I softly reply, motioning for Augustus to let go of Flynn. Augustus may think he can win a fight, but not with a werewolf. Especially to a future Alpha. Flynn could beat him down to a pulp and no one could stand in his way. "Just let Flynn go, he did nothing wrong." Augustus takes in a deep breath, wondering whether to let got of Flynn or cause a fight. If anything Flynn is just watching me, a smirk upon his face, calm and relaxed as he knows he will win anyway. "Augustus, let him-

"Augustus, what's going on here?" Molly shouts, storming over as she grabs her boyfriend's hand, taking it away from Flynn and into her own. Locking their fingers together, she places a soft kiss upon Augustus's cheek, my heart plummeting to the ground. She has him, she know she does, or at least is trying to remind herself.

It seems as if the kiss is not just a statement of possession, but rather a reminder to herself that Augustus is her's. She knows I'm a competitor. We are playing a game, but Augustus should not be a game. We should not be competitions for Augustus. Mates are not just some World Cup game.

"Nothing is going on here," Flynn states, his tone playful as he suddenly wraps an arm around my shoulder. "We are all just peachy."

He knows how to offset Augustus. He knows that Augustus is my mate an he knows how to push those selective buttons. He knows that by displaying a form of possession over me that Augustus will only become pissed. Mate bonds are hard to just switch off and forget that they ever existed. "Doesn't look peachy to me," Molly comments, pulling Augustus a bit farther away from Flynn and me. With Flynn invading my personal space after dropping such a huge bomb, Augustus only keeps his eyes locked upon the two of us, never taking them away.

"We're good," I state, pushing Flynn's arm off of me as I open up the door to my car. "I'll see you guys tomorrow at the graduation rehearsal," I inform, hurting the car door as Molly pulls Augustus away from us and back to their cars. Just as I'm about to speed off, Flynn hops into the passenger seat, causing my blood to boil slightly. "Dude, just because you confessed that you want a relationship with me does not mean that you act like we're almost an item."

Flynn kicks his feet up, putting them upon my dashboard as my eyes widen. Right away I grab my plastic cup that held a smoothie earlier today, lightly slapping his feet. "Not to my baby. Don't leave your dirty footprints upon my baby." Rolling his eyes, Flynn takes his feet down, sitting like a normal individual in the car, going through my radio stations. "What's is all of this about, Flynn?"

"What is what all about?" He asks, settling for a classic rock station that plays in the background.

"Suddenly you just admit feeling for me and I'm expected to let you into my car and place claim over me before my mate?"

Flynn crosses his arms, rolling down the window as I drive off, knowing Flynn will probably just shift from wherever we are and come back for his car. "You remember the day I fought with the human...how you tried to talk it through with me?" I nod. "He made fun of you."

I'm screwed. He's had feelings and I don't want to know how long for. How though? How did I attract the future Alpha? How did the shy girl who faced a mate loving someone else end up causing another to fall for her?

"You don't beat someone up because they poked fun at another person," I calmly state, hoping to not get the future Alpha all rallied up. "Don't beat someone up over me because they make fun on me."

Flynn leans his head against the window, his eyes shutting as I press on the grass a little bit more. My baby speeds up as I hit the light at yellow, wanting to be home as soon as possible. But my parents will either bombard me with questions and details or watch me head up to my room. They know alive needed space lately, but they have no idea why I can't shift.

"I'm sorry."

I raise an eyebrow, taking my eyes from the road briefly to see Flynn looking my way. He just apologized. An apology from a wolf with Alpha blood is rare. It's strange. "What?"

"I'm sorry for beating that douche-

"Not a douche," I interrupt.

"I'm sorry for beating that kid up. Do you forgive me?" Flynn asks, his tone not sharp or demanding anymore, but sincere and peaceful. It's a genuine apology and that's what makes me scared.

"I accept your apology." Flynn responds with a small smile pulling at his lips, one that makes me smile in return. But he's not mine, he is someone else's that will soon claim him. "Well, are you going to run back home or come inside?" I ask, arriving at my house as I see my dad's truck is back from world. Flynn follows my lead, hopping out as well as we head for the front door of the house. Mom practically begged dad to buy this house. Dad wanted a place closer to the pack house and mom fell in love with this place. With four bathrooms, a nice game room, dinning area, and the essential rooms, that wasn't what hooked her, but rather the open rooms filled with windows, the wooden floors, and the garden from the previous owners.

Flynn enters my house, my parents sitting in the living room as we enter. Already I know he will be staying for dinner due to the looks on their faces. Before I know it my mom is pulling Flynn in for a hug and my father raising an eyebrow at me. He thinks something is going on. As mom grabs another plate for dinner and Flynn and my father sit in the living room, talking about an upcoming hunt, I take my place on the steps of the stairs, going through my texts. Augustus tried to reach me while Flynn was apologizing, asking if I would come over for dinner tonight.

"Dinner is ready," mom calls out. With everyone soon seated around the circular table in the dining room, I take ahold of the knife, digging into the stake in the plate as everyone else does as well. I keep up my manors tonight, knowing my dad would scold me for eating fast and like a savage before a guest on the walls of the house. Dad's mom was a manor freak, thankfully my father not taking the same habits when he moved away and soon enough married my mom. "So, Flynn, any plans this summer after graduation?" Mom asks, taking up the first step in conversation as my parents await a reply.

"Pack business and just running free. I'll be attending college, commuting for a business degree." Business. It's cliché how every future Alpha will most likely do business due to running the 'family business.' You need to know how to make treaties, manage money, and so much more as Alpha or even a Beta.

"Sounds interesting," my dad comments, taking a sip of the water upon the table. It's not the most interesting in my opinion, as well as that I know Flynn does not want to do that. Sure, he wants to become Alpha and run the pack, but not for a while. I've known him long enough to know that he wants to study nothing business at all, but rather computer programming. He wants to get a masters in it too, take a break from pack life, and then, when the pack needs him, return and run the pack. He wants to live a normal life a few years first before going back to tradition.

We carry on with the conversation of the year ahead, my mind bored as the subject of pack meetings is brought up. I can tell Flynn is bored as well, judging by how he looks at me with pleading eyes every few seconds or so.

As dinner comes to a close, I find myself watching my parents shoo us out of the room. Flynn follows me down the hall, into my room as I make sure nothing is scattered across the floor that could cause embarrassment. With a clean room before me, I open the door fully, allowing Flynn access as he knows the familiar room. He used to spend nights here after broken-hearted, bags under his eyes, looking like shit, and needing help.

"You don't have to get a business degree, you know," I inform, taking a seat at the futon beside my window. "You're a free person."

Flynn shakes his head. "Not with my parents."

"You're the future Alpha. You're strong. you stand up for what you believe and want," I state. "You don't have to follow their wants, just tell them, I know you want to." Flynn shakes his head, taking a seat beside my desk upon my swivel chair. "They won't be happy but they will understand."

"They won't-

"How do you know?" I question. "You've never tried it before. You follow what they want and don't try it your way. You don't know how they will respond."

"Amory, my parents want me to know how to run a business, the pack," Flynn argues, leaning back in my chair.

I shake my head. "You can tell them that by the time they want you to run the pack, you'll have a degree in business. You'll get your degree in computer programming and work until a certain age, get that business degree, and return to the pack."

Flynn's eyes brows furrow together, frustrated with the idea. We've talked about this before. We've discussed this talk to his parents before and every time, right when he finds his confidence to do so, he backs down. I know his mother, the Luna, a sweetheart who loves her family. His father...he's a tough nut to crack. But get the mother to agree and the father will have to as well. Women are the neck of the house and they can turn the head anyway they want. Simple logic taught by a classic RomCom.

"Promise me something," Flynn adds, causing me to wonder what he's about to ask. I nod. "I'll talk with my parents if you're there with me."

"We've done that before," I point out, remembering how Flynn backed down that time four months ago.

"I'll do it this time, I swear."

"Okay, I'll do it," I agree, holding out my hand for the future Alpha to shake. "Make it a deal."

Getting to his feet, Flynn takes my hand, shaking it as I hold eye contact with him. I'm proud of him, that he's finally taking charge. But he's done it before. I'll tell him how proud I am of him when he actually gets the talk over with.

Just as I'm about to drop my hand, Flynn pulls me up from the futon, holding me close as I find myself in the same situation as yesterday.

"Thank you," he whispers, pulling me in for a hug. "Thank you."

CHAPTER 9

My gown brushes against my fingers, the material feeling itchy around my neck as my name is called. I do the rehearsal walk, doing a quick little walk out of the isle of the row of chairs and back into my seat. Four hundred students and I just have to make it through seventy more until we are through here. In two days I will put on my cords and pins for my gown to be decorated in, my cap decorated with my graduation year, and a lump in my throat. I watch as Augustus walks, doing the rehearsal as I see Molly waving at him. High school sweethearts. Barely anyone knows the drama.

In another ten minutes I'm free from the auditorium, grabbing a drink of the way back home as I need my caffeine. With the radio station Flynn set yesterday still on, I start my drive home, taking a sip of the cold coffee in my hands. My phone rings, my eyes rolling as I set down my coffee and answer the call. "Hello?"

"You never answered me last night."

Augustus is on the line. It's true, I never replied to his invite for dinner last night. After all, Flynn was sitting at my table, chatting up a storm with my parents, laughter occurring, chats of the future, and making me forget that Augustus was in love with someone else.

"I was busy," I respond, pulling into my driveway as my parents are not home yet. "I didn't have the chance to text you back."

Heading into the house, I await Augustus's next words. "How about we meet up for dinner tonight? The diner, in an hour?" The diner is where we would spend hours and hours of our lives talking about school, people, and just life in general. The diner was our place, a place where I opened up to Augustus, where we took me in the first few weeks of our friendship. It was our place...until he took Molly there and made it their place. "You still there, Amory?"

"Yah, I'm still here," I reply, leaning my head against the front door. "Could we eat somewhere else?" I know he's confused now, he's wondering what's wrong. It used to be that I would jump on the idea, not ask for another location like I just have. "I just ate their the other night." It's true, somewhat, as I ate there with my mother the other night.

"Okay, how about I pick up and we'll decide from there?" Augustus suggests, background music playing as I assume he's in his car. Why does he keep pushing for this? No, I'm not mad, but I'm hesitant. Hesitating because he's in a relationship and I knew he's beginning to see me as more than a friend. I don't want to be the girl that interrupts a relationship and only causes drama, but he's my mate. Is it even wise to go and grab dinner with him now? Sure, before all of this mess I would of thought nothing more of it than best friends grabbing a meal, but now it's different. Different because we are mates and he has a girlfriend. A girlfriend that could give him a normal life. "You still there, Amory?"

"Yah, yah I'm still here," I state, scratching the back of my head. Opening the house, I place my items upon the living room couch, going back to giving Augustus a response. "I'll be ready in an hour."

"See you then," Augustus responds, hearing me end the call as I place my phone down. For the next ten minutes I stand by the kitchen table, looking outside as cars pass bye. This is not all a good idea, the idea of heading out for a dinner with Augustus while he has shown signs of something more than a best friend to me. Don't get me wrong, I am overjoyed, but it causes drama. By risking a relationship between Molly and Augustus, I am only causing drama, but I want him. I need him.

He is my mate and there's nothing in heaven or hell that could alter that decision of fate. Augustus is mine, at least he should be mine, not hers. He should be mine and not that female's who has him. Has him on a loose leash because now, Augustus has had a faint feel of what the mate bond can do to a person. Augustus has had a taste of the drug called a mate bond and he will never be able to push it behind him.

Until Augustus arrives, I spend half of the time just laying on my bed, and the rest of the twenty minutes or so staring at the girl in the mirror. She's broken yet she's strong in some ways. There's a piece of her missing, digging a hole deeper into an abyss she may never come out of. That piece of me has been absent much of these past months. I remember the first time he told me that he loved the human female, how he was here, in my room, his eyes brighter than the sun and his smile wider than I'd ever seen. He was happy. He was overjoyed. He was head over heels and swearing to me that she was perfect, yet his perfect girl was standing beside him the entire time.

The doorbell rings, my eyes shifting to the vehicle out front. He's here and I still have to get ready. Sliding into a pair of jeans and cream blouse, I rush down the stairs, grabbing my purse on the way out, opening the door in a hurry to find Augustus just about to knock again. A smile falls upon his face and my heart melts. "Hey, you ready?"

"Yah." Following Augustus out and towards his truck, I grab the door for myself before he can. If anything, I need this night to be one of friendship, not one of a possible spending the night at someone's house. Augustus...When I learned he was my mate, I had wished that I could of taken away the memory of my first night with a boy, to have him be my first. Sex was fun before I met Augustus, and now, now that I know who he is, sex is a constant reminder that my mate has never held me in such a way. Has moved with me in such a way.

"So, burger?" He asks, gaining a nod from me as I set the radio to the station Flynn played the other night. "Since when do you listen to this?" Augustus asks, his tone happy as he meets my gaze.

What do I say? That I had Flynn here and he showed me my new favorite music? The mate bond is taking greater effect now, meaning I have to start being selective of my words.

"Spotify suggested it," I lie, looking out the window as we begin our drive. "How's Molly?"

He's tense. What happened between them? I'm used to him confessing when they have fights. I'm used to him telling me the things he loves about her as well. I'm used to him breaking my heart.

"We had a slight argument yesterday," he explains. I press him on with a raised eyebrow. "She...you know I am telling you this because I trust you, right?" I nod. "She says that I care more for you than a best friend should."

"Augustus-

He pulls over onto the side of the road, turning off the radio as he puts the truck in park. "Do I?" I let him continue talking as I know better than to speak right now. I've seen Augustus like this before, before he confesses something that has been eating him alive. "I know you lied that the kiss meant nothing to you, Amory. I've been your best friend for years and I know a lie when I hear one." My throat becomes dry. "That night, when I texted you that the kiss was just a game, a dare, that was a lie as well." I know what he means.

Leaning forward, Augustus searches my eyes for any type of signal, any detail he is missing. "I need you to hear me out, Augustus," I whisper, my mind running blank as he awaits my next words. "I cannot be the side chick or the girl that causes drama to unfold within a relationship." He nods.

"What do you feel? What do you feel for me?"

Tears begin to brim, close to letting loose as I can feel all the pent-up anger and sadness wanting to be let free. I want to unleash all the emotions I've locked away for months and months.

"Augustus, I cannot break Moll-

"This is your chance, Amory. This is your one chance to tell me the truth and tell me what is really going on in that head of yours."

"Or?"

"Or you can be a coward and I will forget that we even have a possibility for something greater."

I know what I have to do. I know what must be done here.

"Amory?"

A tear escapes, letting me know I have to tell him what I must.

"That kiss...this whole thing we have going, Augustus..." I pause, watching as he leans in closer. "I-I don't want you as a friend anymore, but-

I'm cut off, lips pressed against mine as I welcome them in, pulling him closer to me. My fingers run through his blond hair, the locks thick as I hold him closer, his hand on the back of my neck as he makes sure I do not back away.

Sparks. Sparks is all I can feel as I thirst for more and more. My wolf begins to surface, a tingling beginning in my fingers as I haven't felt my wolf surface in months like this.

As he pulls away, his eyes peeling open slowly as I do the same, my gaze locked with his own. I did it. I admitted.

"Amory?" A slight blush creeps up and onto my cheeks. "I want you more than I have ever wanted anything in the world. I want a relationship with you not of just best friends, but something more." I smile. "I want the simple intimacy of holding hands, of looking into your eyes as I wake up or go to bed, to kiss you without caring who sees, and to hold you as if the world is falling apart around us and all we have is one another."

"August-

"Amory, will you let me? Will you let us... have this?"

I seal my decision, pulling in Augustus for another kiss as my wolf feels alive within me. A smile traces my lips as they are pressed against his own, one I cannot contain as I pull away from the kiss. "Believe me, Augustus, I want this as well," I comment, pulling him back in as a set of hunter green eyes flash through my mind. Flynn is going to be pissed.

CHAPTER 10

Am I the mistress? You read about them or watch them in the news, how they tear apart a couple and it never ends well. You see how they are given tons of publicity and people turn their heads from them. Am I the mistress now? Sure, this is high school, only high school, but high school never leaves you, especially when you're a werewolf. As a wolf, your pack is your family, and when plenty of your pack members are at the same school as you, especially your mate, high school is more than just a chapter in your life. High school is when you become that warrior you wanted, you becomes besties with the Alpha, date an omega, and countless other possibilities. It's where you make your mark on who you will become as part of the pack. If you're vital....or nothing more than a member. To Augustus and Molly, high school is just those for years of your life and then you move on. To them, it's just a memory.

"Amory?"

Am I the mistress?

"What's next for us, Augustus?" I ask, leaning my head back against the headrest. He still keeps his eyes focused upon me, turned to face me as we are still parked on the side of the road. It's a quite road, one many only travel when going to or from school. "Molly is your girlfriend."

"We're on a break," he explains, turning down the radio. "We are about to graduate anyway, Amory, what are we worried about? The crowd of high school? The drama?" He's human, high school, once it's done, it's done. For me, high school sets you up in the food chain for your place in the pack. "If what we have is right, if what we have is true, that we both feel these things for one another, then what is in our way?"

I know what he means. We have nothing in our way. But then again, as relating to pack business, what would having a relationship with Augustus place me as to my pack? What would my pack see me as? Weak? How could they see me as weak as I am simply claiming my mate? I think it's my respect for myself. I do not want to be the girl that tore a couple apart even if we are mates.

"Tell me, Amory, what stands in our way? What is keeping us from a beautiful relationship?"

"Nothing," I reply, watching as a smile crosses across Augustus's lips, my heart fluttering. Nothing but the fact that I will also have to tell him one day. One day I will have to expose him to a world filled with creatures his kind calls monsters. They makes movies and shows off of our kind, depicting us as wild being that have to be slaughtered. As it ever occurred to the humans, that the only monster out there, is those who kill us for the fun. They do not kill to protect, they kill for game.

"Still want dinner?" Augustus asks, his eyes scanning my face as I agree.

Within ten minutes we've arrived at a small burger joint, grabbing food as we talk the hour away. We talk about old memories, about ones that made us laugh or cry. We discuss the event of us meeting, how that day we became best friends. But we stay clear of Molly. We stay clear of all of that. I wish I could tell him about the time I discovered he was my mate. I wish I could unleash the emotions and tell him how much I wanted to run away because I saw him look at her when I was right beside him. Augustus has confessed his love for Molly...is love that hard to love ahold of? He was content with her weeks ago and now they are falling apart? What's going on? Fate perhaps?

As we finish up our meal, I watch as he smiles, how the creases form around his eyes, how his eyes light up, how his pearly white teeth are on display. I watch his smile as if the most beautiful thing I have ever witnessed. How have I gone on for so long suffering?

Back in his truck, the radio surrounds us as we are left to our thoughts. Tonight was fun, it was not a mistake nor something I will look back on and cringe. Tonight was the night I told Augustus my feeling and he didn't not push me away, because he had those feelings as well. "What about Molly?"

Augustus sighs. "I need to let her know. I need to tell her about this, about us," he explains, taking the familiar rode back to my place. He's right to do so, to let Molly know, but I don't want to watch her break. I don't want to watch her fall apart like I did. But she's human, she will never be able to feel what I feel for Augustus because he is not her mate. Because she's not his mate, she will get over him. One day she will let him go, but it will be hard. I feel awful knowing she will feel miserable. "Better now than later. It's my job to inform her, not a friend or classmate." I agree.

"Do what is best," I add, agreeing with Augustus as we pull up before my house. The lights are off, my mother's car absent as well as my father's. They said they would be gone at a pack meeting, a dinner with the Alpha and his Elders. As the car comes to a stop, Augustus turns off the engine, rushing around to my door before I can open it. "Thank you." Augustus shuts the door behind me, sliding an arm around my waist as we walk side by side to the front door. Sparks fly everywhere as all it takes is a simple touch, my body electrified as I know Augustus feels it as well. It's just a matter of time before he brings up the topic. The only question is, will I be able to tell him? Tell him what he is entitled to know.

Digging through my purse, I search for my keys, rummaging through the leather object as my eyes widen.

"Shit."

"Are you locked out?" Augustus asks, a playful tone in his voice as I roll my eyes as I watch him. "Let's find an unlocked window or see if the back door it either." Little does he know I could just grow out my claws and open the door. It's simple for a wolf to break in without any sign of violence or damage.

Taking my hand, Augustus leads me over to the fence, smiling as I know this will be another memory. It may not seem like much, but one day we will look back on it as one of our first adventures. Letting go of my hand, he holds out his hands as they are locked together. "Step onto my hands and I'll hoist you up to climb the fence."

Doing as Augustus instructs, I just want to show off, to show my skills, how I can easily jump this fence like its nothing. As my hands reach the top of the fence, I pull myself up, shifting my body to the other side of the fence as I see the backyard before me. Once my feet hit the grass, I wait ten seconds before Augustus is over, walking beside me as we head for the back door. Taking out his wallet, Augustus grabs a credit card, sliding it between the door and doorway, hearing a click as we are in. "Are your parents home?"

Shaking my head, I turn on the kitchen lights, setting my purse down as Augustus locks the back door. "Out for another hour or two I suppose. Dinner at a old friend's place." It's not a lie, it's a vague term to use for Flynn's family.

Arms wrap around me, pulling me into a hard chest as his lips are pressed against my temple. I know he's no stranger to the world of 'romance,' as I've felt the pain every time he had sex with Molly. Every time he had it, I felt a pain at the pit of my stomach, it felt as if it was eating me alive as it made its way up to my heart. Bruises would form in the morning and I would have to remind myself that Augustus had no idea what he was doing. He as no idea that having sex with Molly would hurt me in ways I can never forget.

"Tell me something," I whisper, leaning my head back upon his shoulder.

"What?" He asks, taking me down playfully onto the couch in the living room. As we sit beside one another, I spit something moving in the shadows outside. Something not good lurks in the backyard, watching us, and I know it won't be good tomorrow.

"Why did you talk to me that day, years ago?"

He knows what I'm referring to: the day he talked to me and we become best friends.

"Some would call it fate I assume," he begins. It's true, fate had a major play, as we are mates. "But it was your smile. It was soft and kind, one that let me know you were someone I could trust in and find loyal."

I find myself smiling, watching as he leans forward, pressing a soft kiss upon my lips as my eyes shut.

A howl fills the night sky. I should of pulled the curtain shut.

CHAPTER 11

"**A**re you sure?"

"I promised you I would. I will not break a promise," I confirm, grabbing his arm. Pulling the future Alpha back from the door, I take in a deep breath. "You asked for my help and I promised I would help you." Flynn nods, trying to relax as I can tell he is nervous. "Let's go."

He nods, placing his hands in his pockets as time begins to run out. After all, in two hours I walk down the rows of chairs and receive my diploma. For now, I am at the front door of Flynn's place, the massive double doors awaiting the two of us. I've been here multiple times, for pack meeting or dinners with the Alpha's family. It's a blessing to be invited here. However, I'm not here for good terms with the Alpha and Luna, as I am about to aid their son in telling them off. To let him control his future and not be subject to their decisions for him.

I want to bring up something with Flynn, something that refers to the other night. A single wolf howl that filled the air let me know that Flynn had seen what went on. He saw what happened, he was there when Augustus and I concluded that we no longer wanted to be apart. Hell, this morning Augustus drove over to Molly's house, calling me afterwards to inform me that they were no more. Molly and Augustus are on an official break, broken up as I feel all the blame. I broke apart two individuals, but she was never his to begin with.

"Ready?" I ask, removing my hand from Flynn's arm as the hunter green eyes follow my actions. Reaching for the handle upon the the door, I motion for Flynn to follow. Flynn nods, straightening out his black shirt as he's nervous, watching as the door fully opens. The first steps I take across the white, marble floors, they echo in the grant entrance, a circular room before me as a staircase lines the walls. Archways lead to three different rooms, each with polished mahogany floors, chandeliers in each one as I wonder where his parents are.

"Kitchen," Flynn explains, motioning to the left archway where a massive dinning room is located. Entering the room, I'm presented the long table, perfectly placed chairs around the table, and a Persian rug under. With a doorway to the left, Flynn makes a short stop. "I'll go in first," he comments, taking in a deep breath as I offer him a gentle smile.

Heading in after Flynn, I see his parents, the Alpha and Luna, sitting at the table beside marble cabinets. "Amory, what a surprise dear," Luna Willow greets, her pearly whites on display as she gets to her feet. Dressed in pastel pink, she looks stunning, her jet black hair pulled into a sleek ponytail, and her hazel eyes meeting mine. "Cade, come and greet Amory," she tells her husband and Alpha, the male sitting with his back to us as he looks out the massive window.

The Alpha looks around, his blond hair looking like gold in the sunlight, his dark green eyes resembling Flynn's, and his build tall and built. Flynn used to talk of his father as if the best man alive; that was until two years ago when Flynn got back from a hunt on rogues. Flynn was injured and in his time of medical attention, a rogue escaped, his father beyond enraged as he was given a lesson before all the training warriors in the pack. I wasn't there, but I hear Alpha Cade let his Beta show Flynn what happens when you let someone escape, how he landed punch after punch on the sophomore. Due to that, I understand why Flynn does not speak fondly of his father. His mother is another story, how she fought with her husband that night and forced him to apologize to not only Flynn, but the entire pack.

"What do we owe the pleasure?" Alpha Cade asks, getting to his feet as I already feel intimidated. "I hear you two are-

"We need to talk," Flynn interrupts his father, looking to me as I nod.

"Flynn, sweetie, do you find your..." I know what Luna Willow is trying to say, to ask. She wants to know if he's found his mate.

A lump forms in my throat as Flynn begins his talk. "I don't want to go to college to major in business."

"Are you saying you don't want to be Alpha?" Alpha Cade snaps, raising his voice as my eyes widen. He's mad. "That you are willing to throw out your pack for the sake of your selfish reasons and forget about your kin!" I watch as Flynn tenses, how his jaw clench-es, how his posture stiffens, and his eyes harden. "You cannot be serious!"

"Hear me out," Flynn demands, slamming his first onto the kitchen table, the wood shattering as I jump back. That table was

not made of cheap wood. Not at all. "I want to get a different degree first." No interruptions. "I want to work that job for a matter of years, and when you want to pass down the title of Alpha, I will get a business degree and take over." He's trying to remain calm. He's trying not to shift and demand the respect he deserves. Two individuals with Alpha blood going head to head is never a good combination. It's a deadly recipe.

"You listen to me, son," Cade growls. "You will go to college. You will graduate. You will get a business degree."

I watch Luna Willow, watching as she moves to her husband's side, tugging upon his arm to have him sit. "I will get a business degree when you need me to take over the pack. Alphas don't retire till they can fight no longer, father, and you have another twelve years on you to run this pack. In twelve years I swear I will have that business degree to run the pack when you hand it over to me."

Flynn is trying to calm down, how he straying to steady his breathes. Luna Willow sits next to her husband, rubbing his arm as I can tell his wolf is close to unleashing. "Mom, what do you think?"

He needs me here because he wants to be strong. I've done this before with him, I was by his side as he asked out his first big crush in eighth grade, I was by his side as girls left him heartbroken, and I am now by his side as he stands up to his parents. I've been his cornerstone for when he needs the extra strength.

"What degree, Flynn?" Luna Willow asks, her eyes briefly meeting my own. She's scared of what her husband could do today. She's scared something could happen that could leave their family broken more than ever. There are parts of this family not even their best friends could even know. I've seen much of it. I know what goes on in this household. I know more than the family secret of the deceased Olive, Flynn's older sister and the true future Alpha of this pack. She died seven years ago, at fourteen, a werewolf killed in a car accident. Luna Willow was in the car, driving, Flynn in the backseat, and Olive arguing with her mother about a boy. Flynn and Luna Willow made it, Olive did not.

T-boned by a truck, Olive did not make it as she died before the ambulance could arrive. Flynn once told me about it one night, how his mother could not set foot in another car for months, how his father lost hold upon the family, and Flynn was told he had to become Alpha.

"Computer programming," Flynn states, interrupting my thoughts as I realize something that I never felt. His hand is in mine, our fingers interlocked as his hand shakes. "Four year degree and I have scholarships from private companies to get that degree. I'm good at it and love it." He wants to break tradition of this pack, of what being the future Alpha means.

Luna Willow nods, bowing her head as Alpha Cade let's out a deep sigh. "Cade?" She asks, facing her husband as I feel Flynn hold my hand tighter.

He never wanted to be told to be the next Alpha. Life to him was once that he was to live a more normal life. He was to not be forced to do things that set him on a path to becoming the Alpha. Most don't see it, but I do. I see the future Alpha who is afraid of running a pack because he does not want to do it. Hell, it may be surprising, but Flynn is graduating first in class in a matter of hours. Flynn even tutored students in math and science, taking their grades from C's and D's to A's.

"What do you think, Amory?" Alpha Cade asks, his tone harsh as my throat becomes dry. He's asking me to give my opinion on a family issue. On an issue that could change the Alpha's opinion of me forever.

"Don't bring her into this," Flynn growls, his Alpha tone on display as I want to get out of here. "This is a family issue-

"Yet you brought her into the family issue," Alpha Cade snaps, getting to his feet as Luna Willow looks to me. She feels sorry for me to be involved in this family affair. I know more than she thinks I know. Flynn's told me about the other women, about how his father has brought mistresses into their beach house or even here, sleeping with them, giving them gifts of diamonds. Luna Willow is not blind to it, but she knows her pack comes first. She's a wise woman stuck with an asshole.

"Mother?" Flynn asks, ignoring his father now as he wants only his mother's approval. I don't blame him, his mother is the true figurehead to respect here.

Luna Willows nods. "I say do it. If you love it, go and do it."

Alpha Cade growls. "We will not find your tuition," he snaps, his tone outraged as Flynn pulls me closer to his side.

"I don't need your money. The college has given me a full ride." I watch as Luna Willow nods her head, knowing that Flynn has his heart set out upon his dream. One of the first times I saw him at school, he was surrounded by silence, in his own little world as his headphones were on and he was typing away. At the time I had no idea what he was up to, later on I found out he had hacked into the school's a tendency system. "This is my dream."

Alpha Cade turns his attention to me once more, his eyes turning black as I become afraid. I'm afraid that he will turn me rogue, he will make me an omega, that he will do something negative to my family name. "Do you respect your parents, Amory?"

"I do, Sir," I reply calmly, my insides turning to jelly as I become afraid.

"Do you believe they have your best interests at heart?"

"You don't care about my interests," Flynn snaps before I can even reply.

"I believe that they know what I want and respect that." I have to stay calm. If I lose my cool, who knows what else in this house could become like the table. "They may not agree with me, but they know I am wise with what I choose."

Alpha Cade nods his head, walking over to the other side of the kitchen, behind the marble counters as he grabs a beer from the fridge. "Tell me, Flynn, do you even care for this pack?"

"That's enough, Cade, damn it!" Luna Willow shouts, rising to her feet as the clicking of her heels envelops the silence of the room. "Flynn and Amory, go." Flynn nods, taking my arm as he pulls me with him. "We will discuss and come up with an answer by tomorrow. Go get ready to graduate."

We exit the kitchen, Flynn excusing himself for a brief minute as he has to go and grab his clothes for the ceremony. He does not plan on staying here any longer than needed. I watch as he rushes up the stairs, telling me that if I hear any more yelling, to go and wait by his car. In five minutes he's back, changed into a suit as Flynn looks sharp, the suit fitting his build well. With the blue robe and cap in his hands, he rushes back down the stairs, opening the front door for me as the sunlight greets my eyes. Piling into his car, the familiar station is on as I know that I've come to think of Flynn whenever I flip by the stations. Everyday, when I go through the stations, I'll come across the classic rock, I stop and listen. I think of Flynn, of how he will tap is fingers to the beat, how he bobs his head, how he will allow a ghost smile to cross his lips.

"Amory?"

"Yah?" I ask, snapping back into what is going on. My eyes widen to find Flynn leaning in, his lips inches from my own as my heartbeat quickens. "Flynn?"

"Amory," he whispers, closing the distance as Augustus passes my mind. I'm with my mate, with Augustus now.

Shoving the future Alpha away, I watch as he holds a questioned look upon his face. "What's going on?" He asks, raising an eyebrow.

"I-I'm with Augustus."

The spark in his eyes falls, fading away into a dullness as a thin line forms at his lips. "The other night, you were there. I heard you howl when he was back at my place. You know we are together and I'm sorry, but I've chosen him."

He shakes his head. "You chose him because he is only your mate!"

My blood begins to boil. "Yes, he is my mate, but I love him. Even without the mate bond I love him."

Flynn shakes his head, putting the car in drive as he speeds off. "Keep telling yourself that." A form pulls at my lips as Flynn speeds through the minutes, the radio off, the soft pure of the engine now an annoying sound, and all I want is to arrive at school and get out of this car.

As we come to the parking lot of the school, I spot my Prius parked beside his car. I still have to chance into my cap and gown, my dress already on, the white material hitting my mid-thigh, my nude heels tall, and my hair curled. I'm dressed for a good time, not for an emotional day of sadness. Just as Flynn is about to open his mouth to speak again, I spot Augustus, walking to where Flynn is parked. "Here's your boyfriend now."

He's not happy with me.

Opening the door, the second my heels meet the pavement, Augustus is by my side. "Hello, Flynn," Augustus greets, glaring at the future Alpha as I am uncertain of what they are about to do. Wrapping an arm over my shoulder, Augustus pulls me away, placing a kiss upon my forehead as my heart skips a beat.

"Amory!" Looking over my shoulder, I spot Flynn, putting his cap on. "Thank you...for my parents."

I smile. "You're welcome."

I cannot let this get out of hand.

Chapter 12

Arms wrap around me, a soft kiss placed upon my cheek as a smile stretches across my lips. Holding my diploma closer, I turn my head to the side, meeting his lips as we close the space between us. Pulling away, I pull Augustus in for a hug, adjusting my cap as my mother takes a quick photo.

"Mom!"

"You two are just too adorable," she comments, winking playfully at me as I know what she's up to. She does this a bit: embarrassing her daughter for some well done memories. She knows I hate pictures, especially with a boy. I told her and my father the other night about Augustus, how we decided to be a couple. I also told her we were mates but that I will wait until the correct time to tell him about what we are. About what I am. My parents respect my decision to wait to tell him, to wait until things get more serious between the two of us before I reveal to him a world of, as the humans see it, monsters. "Amory, don't go off yet," mother snaps playfully at me as I'm about to head to a group of friends.

Augustus laughs, kissing my cheek for one last photo before we head off, waving to my mom as he takes my hand. "Graduated kids now," Augustus comments, smiling at me as my heart softens at his smile. "All free until college." College. I am going to forget that word even exists as I want to live in the moment with Augustus. I have my mate now and I am content. "Let's take a trip sometime."

"Where?" I ask, walking around the corner with Augustus as we are out of out sight. Pulling me in for a quick kiss, I wrap my arms around his neck, pulling myself onto my tiptoes as Augustus gently pushes me against the wall.

Pulling back, Augustus tilts his head, looking down upon me. "Anywhere. The beach, the mountains, hell, even the flat lands of Kansas. You name it and we will go."

I smile, grabbing ahold of Augustus's collar on his gown, pulling him closer to me as I bite my lip. "How about we just take a day t-

"Amory?"

"Yah?" I ask Augustus, raising an eyebrow as he interrupted me when I have him a reply.

"Could you excuse me a second, just hold onto your reply," Augustus whispers, turning his head to the left as I see her. She's beautiful as always, her ginger hair curled to her shoulders, her gown unzipped as her beautiful peach dress is on display. She's watching us, biting her lower lip, her eyes moving between Augustus and me. "Sorry." I nod, watching as he leaves the secluded hallway and walks over to his ex. I know he still feels something for him. It's been barely even two days since they split, there's no way in hell Augustus could just be over her by now. It will take time.

I watch as he talks to her, how he stuffs his hands in his pockets and greets her with a friendly smile. She simply offers a lopsided smile back, rubbing her arms as she's uncomfortable. I know she is. I don't blame her for being uncomfortable. She's not happy with his decision, and if anything, she's pissed with me.

"Amory?" Turning around, my eyes widen to see Luna Willow before me, dressed no longer in pastel pink, but a creme dress that hits her knees, a beautiful pearl necklace upon her necklace, and in those eyes. That beautiful eyes now dull due to all the hell she has put up with over the years. "Congratulations on your diploma," she states, pulling me in for a short hug. "My apologies for the situation a little bit ago, I'm sorry you had to see all of that."

I nod. "I forgive you, I understand that as a mother you are looking out for your son."

"It's more Cade than anything...I'm sorry, it's not my rightful place to share information about my problems of marriage." I understand what she's saying, how it's out of place to tell a teenager and pack member how difficult your husband can be. I've seen how they act around the pack, how you would think them to be the perfect couple. "I wanted to also thank you." I raise an eyebrow. "You're strong to come before Cade and support Flynn on that subject. It takes a lot of strength for a pack mate to stand up to an Alpha."

I don't know what to say exactly. "Thank you," I reply to all of that, looking quickly over my shoulder to see Augustus and Molly no longer alone, but green eyes himself beside the two of them. He's causing drama, unwanted drama that I know he's foolish to seek. He doesn't like Augustus and I together and wants to make it a clear point. "If you don't mind, I have to go back to a conversation..."

"Oh, don't let me keep you. I have to leave now anyway, have a good day, Anory," Luna Willow states, walking away after a short hug.

Turning back to the group, I don't like how he stands there, hands in pockets as if causal, a smirk placed across his lips. He's trouble and he knows it pretty damn well. Pacing myself over to the three, the group becomes four as I join, meeting his gaze with a short glare. I want him to leave this all alone, I want him to acknowledge that I am with my mate and that he is simply my Alpha. He will find his mate one day, he will forget me, he will move on and leave the memories of us in the past as his mate is his world. "Flynn," I greet, my none negative as Molly glances at me with the same connotation. "Good valedictorian speech." It is true, how Flynn made a beautiful speech upon the 'minds of the future' and what you are used to hearing at a graduation. The future is before us now, and the four of us each have our own future.

"Thank you," Flynn remarks, nodding to me as I force a small smile onto my face as I turn to Molly. How do I even face the girl who lost her boyfriend because of me? "I was just discussing with Augustus and Molly about next year. Did you know Augustus plans to be halfway across the country?"

I know what he's doing here. I know that Flynn is bringing up how Augustus will be far away in months and that, because of that, we will struggle. "Not too far," Augustus adds, facing me as he tries to assure me it's not too far.

"Only coming home for winter break and summer I assume?"

"Actu-

"Let's just talk about something other than the future for one," I interrupt, trying to change the subject. I try and make my tone playful, hoping that no one realizes that I hate the subject. "Moll y...I heard you sister flew in from Greece." She nods, explaining to me that her sister is here for another week with her husband and then will be back in Europe.

"You know, Amory," Flynn begins, causing eyes to fall onto the two of us again as my heart skips a beat. "Remember when your parents went to Greece for a week?" A scowl quickly passes across my lips. I remember too well, how Luna Willow would come and check in on me every day. It was freshmen year, and I had finally been bumped up another size in bra. I had forgotten to take my laundry up only for Flynn and his mother to walk in on me, a bright yellow bra with doughnuts as the pattern. Flynn made fun of me the next time he saw me, playfully poking fun as I am still embassies to this day.

"What happened?" Augustus asks, cocking an eyebrow. I know what Flynn is trying to do, how he wants it to sound worse than it actually is and make Auguatus uncomfortable.

"Let's just say Amory-

"Laundry incident," I blurt out, my cheeks becoming tinted as I turn to Augustus. "You ready to head out?"

"I need to just find my mom really quick," Augustus answers, nodding to Molly as they know they must depart for now. "Let's go."

"You go find you mom, I'll walk Amory to her car," Flynn informs, looking to me as I give him a short glare. He needs to know that he cannot just come here and try to get his way. I am with my mate and he should respect that, not try and terrorize us. Augustus nods, waving bye to me as he heads off to find his mother, disappearing into the crowd. Looking back to Flynn, I shake my head.

"I can walk myself out just fine," I mutter, crossing my arms as I watch Flynn roll his eyes.

"Just let me walk you out." If it gets him off of my back I'll do it. Taking in a deep breath, I nod, passing the future Alpha to the exit. With him following close behind me, I pace myself, trying to remind myself to stay calm as I think of Augustus. I finally have my mate. I've suffered for so long and now I have him, loving me, with me as we are as we are supposed to be: together. "Amory?"

Raising an eyebrow, I look over my shoulder to the future Alpha, wondering what he wants. "Amory, I know you have wanted Augustus for months, for months since you discovered he was your mate," he pauses, taking out his keys. "Could that be blind to what is happening? Do you really think that Augustus wants you?"

I stop in my tracks, my blood boiling as I meet his green gaze. "Excuse me."

"He's been practically in love with that red-headed girl for months and suddenly just leaves her for his best friend!" My lips form a firm line, my wolf growling from within the hole she's dug herself into. "Why does he suddenly give that up?"

"Because we're mates," I hiss, feeling my canines extend as Flynn shakes his head.

"It takes time to do what he did, not a fucking day or so."

My hands turn to fists.

"You don't know anything about mates!" I growl. "You don't know what it is like to watch your mate fall helplessly in love with someone else. You don't know that pain. Because you do not know the power of a mate bond, you will never be able to understand that Augustus chose me so fast."

Flynn slides his hands into his pockets. "You're right, I don't have a mate."

"So lay off of mine. When you find her you will know what I am experiencing," I snap, storming off from Flynn. Getting into my car, I hit the gas, forgetting to wait for Augustus as I speed out of the parking lot.

The music. The song.

This is one of Flynn's favorites, one he will smile to while singing along with, tap his fingers to on the wheel, and look at me from time to time with a smile.

I slam my hand on the radio button, surrounding myself in silence as my eyes begin to tear up. How could he be so rude? So careless? So miserable to deal with just because he cannot understand what a mate bond feels like?

I stop my car, locking the vehicle as I place my keys behind a stone. Getting behind a thick area of trees, I strip off my clothes, focusing on the earth before me. I focus on the smell of the fresh mud, the ground below, the sound the laws make while against the ground, and how the wind feels through your coat. Closing my eyes, I take in a deep breath, focusing upon a color.

My bones snap. My muscles pull and stretch. My teeth become sharp and kind. My skin becomes a fur coat.

I shift into my wolf.

CHAPTER 13

"You just have to listen for five minutes," mom says as I enter in through the door. Right away I raise an eyebrow, peering around the corner to see her in the kitchen, looking at me, my father sitting beside her. "You're not in trouble."

"What's going on?" I ask, taking a seat at the table as my eyes move between my parents. Just two hours ago I was asleep in bed, an hour ago I had gone for a run, and now I am wondering what is happening. I went for a run for an hour, loving the feeling I thought that I had forgotten until yesterday when I shifted for the first time in months.

Mom gently smiles at me, taking a seat beside me as I wonder if something is horribly wrong. "We wanted to talk to you about next week." I nod. "The pack wants more kids your age to train over the next two weeks. Nothing bad, but simple training."

I know what this is. It's not bad. It's not normal either. Basically it's a bunch of freshly graduated seniors are brought to the pack house, live there for two weeks, and train with the warriors of the pack. They do this because they know many of us will be heading out into the real world and will need protection. It won't just be humans at our colleges, but vampires, witches, and the whole Scooby gang and such.

"Do you want to do it?"

"They don't really give you a choice, mom," I reply with a smile as she nods. The pack doesn't give you a choice. You have to do it. The only thing is, I'll be away from Augustus for two weeks and will not be able to tell him where I am at all. I'll have to lie to my mate until I can show him my world. Another downside to all of this: Flynn will be there too, and because he's the Alpha's next in line, Flynn will be the 'club president' for the two weeks. If anything, these next two weeks could cause my world to flip upside down and inside out.

"I know, just wanted to give you the heads up," she informs, looking to my father as he gets up from the table.

"Plus there's a pack meeting about it tomorrow morning," my father adds in, placing a kiss upon my mom's check as he heads into his office. Looking to my mother, I watch as she moves through the kitchen, letting me know that there is no further comments onto the conversation.

"I'm going out with Augustus tonight just so you know," I call to my mother. She looks up from the sink, smiling at me.

"He's lucky to have a girl like you."

"I don't know when I'll tell him," I inform, taking a seat. "He doesn't know anything yet. I don't know when I'll have to drop that on him."

"Take your time. Humans are tricky, but I know, Amory," she begins, "I know deep down that the mate bond is strong between you, and when you drop that heavy of a bomb, he will stay."

"Thank you," I reply, hearing a car pull up outside. "I've got to go, Auguatus just got here." She nods, wishing me a good time as I pull on my shoes, grabbing my purse. Heading for the door, my father tells me to be smart, as the second I pull open the door, Auguatus stands before me. His smile makes my heart pound within my chest, his eyes meeting my own as a smile spreads across my face. "Hey," I whisper, tucking a strand of hair behind my ear, tilting my head to the side as he reaches out his hand.

"You ready?"

"Yup," I respond, taking his hand as the sparks fly, electrifying my body as I follow him. With his car before me, I know where we are going tonight, a place that we used to go months ago before Molly stepped into the picture and my heart was broken. "So, how long of a drive?" I ask, sliding into the passenger seat as he opens the door for me.

"About forty minutes," he responds, getting into the driver's seat as the car seems off to me. I'm used to the Italian leather, not because it's nicer or it makes me feel expensive, but because it welcomes me. It's not because it's a nicer car, but because I feel more welcomed in a way, more familiar. The music that plays feels odd, feels off from the usual. "Do you want to pick up food before or after?"

I snap back to the conversation, to reality, to what matters right now. "Whenever really." I have to tell him that I'll be gone next week and the week after that. I'll be in town, but he won't be able to know. I already decided on telling him I'm heading up to visit my Aunt Karen four hours away.

"How do you feel about a weekend getaway?" Augustus asks as he places the blanket down on the bed of the truck. With the movie about to begin at the drive-in, I rub my hands together, looking around the open land where other cars have parked more close to the screen. "Like somewhere out of town? An hour or two away?"

"I'd like that," I reply, picking up the pizza from the seat as the bed of the truck is all set up for the movie. "But it will have to wait," I inform, placing the pizza box on the mattress as Augustus holds out his hand for me to take. Helping me up to the bed of the truck, I take my seat, a pillow against my back as Augustus follows me. With the smell of pizza in the air and the screen bright as the movie plays, Augustus takes ahold of my hand, placing a kiss upon the top as I smile.

"Why does it have to wait?" He asks, grabbing a slice of the pizza as I follow in pursuit.

"I'm going to be gone for two weeks as of next Wednesday. I'm going to an Aunt's about two hours away." Augustus nods, wrapping an arm around my shoulder as he takes in the new information. If only I could tell the truth, if only I could tell him what and where I will be. That I will be around Flynn for hours every day. Flynn, the boy who thinks he has a right to try and terminate my relationship with my mate. The boy who thinks he can get with me when I have a mate. He doesn't understand mates and he won't understand Augustus and me until he finds his mate.

After a good hour and a half movie, I lay beside Augustus, my head on his shoulder, legs intertwined, and my eyelids heavy. "Amory?" I raise an eyebrow as Augustus motions to my side. "Phone." My phone is vibrating on the blanket, a familiar number flashing across the screen as my fingers shake. Moving fast, I deny the call, watching the screen go black as I know he won't be happy.

Hell, for all I know he could make these next two weeks a living hell all because he would rather be with me than me be with him.

I won't let him spoil a date night.

For another twenty minutes we lay the same way, beside one another as the night sky displays hundreds upon hundreds of stars. "Augustus?" He turns to face me, raising an eyebrow as I say his name. Pulling him in for a kiss, my arms wrapping around his neck as I pull him closer than ever. His hands are placed upon my hips, pushing me gently down upon the blanket as he climbs over me. Luckily for us, we parked far away from the other cars, secluded as we are given time to ourselves. "Augustus," I whisper, out of breath as I gently hold him back. "How do you feel about us?"

"What?"

"How do you feel about us?" I state again, holding myself up upon my elbows as he places a hand upon my cheek.

"How do I feel about us? The most amazing girl in the world?" He asks, cocking his head to the side. "The most amazing girl in the world with me, by my side as I get to hold her and tell her how I feel? Amory, when I'm with you, I feel...I feel alive. Every time I see you I feel myself become alive." I smile, pulling him in for a short kiss. "Every time I'm around you, I feel as if I'm no longer searching for the missing piece of a puzzle, but everything is in place."

This time he pulls me in, his hand lightly cupping my cheek as his lips press against mine. I'm back against the blanket, Augustus hovering over me as the movie rolls the credits, cars beginning to turn on to leave.

"Can I ask you something?" Augustus asks, pulling away after we both need to breathe. "About Flynn." A scowl crosses my lips. He knows this is not the best subject and he agrees. "Do you like him?"

My skin pales as my heart skips a beat. Shaking my head, I offer Augustus a soft smile. "Believe me, Augustus, if I liked Flynn, I would not be here with you because that would do no justice to you," I explain, weaving a hand through my hair, the soft sound of a song playing over the speakers the movie once did. I've heard this song, one that I watched Flynn sing along to.

Augustus nods, laying back down as he received his answer. "I like you a lot, Augustus," I begin, turning to face him. "More than a lot, and Flynn has no chance with me because to me he's just an old family friend."

Augustus nods, kissing me softly as I close my eyes once again, knowing that what I have just said, I could never swear by it.

Chapter 14

My duffle bag is loaded, my hair pulled back in a braid as the wind is fierce today. With my change of clothes, a few running shoes, and one formal outfit for the closing night of the two weeks, I have everything that I will need. My phone is secured in my pocket, on silent as my parents have discussed with me how the pack warriors take away our phones the first night. No electronics because we have to become more 'in tune with nature.' These two weeks are basically training, a bit of social anxiety, eating, and sleeping as we are cut off from the outside world except for the electricity and AC within the pack house. Don't get me wrong, the pack house is not some random log cabin locked in the middle of no where. Although it's smack in the middle of the forest of our pack's territory, the house is massive, a huge dining hall, living area, entrance, and tons of bedrooms. Only werewolves were hired to design and build the house as it contains passageways, extra rooms that only the Alpha and the elders know about, and tons of bedrooms the size of college dorms.

"Just be safe and don't break a bone," my mother states, kissing my forehead as my father hops into the truck. He'll be dropping me off and leaving me for two weeks. It sucks. The only people who actually live at the pack house are the pack warriors, a few elders, the doctor, and the Alpha whenever he's going through a workaholic phase. "Love you."

"Love you too," I reply, hopping into the truck as we leave for the pack house, a good thirty minutes through a thick forest and a dirt road.

Within that time, the pack house is before us, a gate opening as our car rolls through, traveling up the private drive as the brick road is under the tires now. Before my eyes lays a beautiful manner, modern architecture as the windows and wide and tall, the house open, the double doors of the entrance pulled open, the white stone having some vibes traveling up to the third floor, and other cars as well unloading as I recall people from my newly graduated class. Maybe I'll get lucky and these two weeks will be fun, or maybe they will be like hell as I am separated from my mate.

As I unload and grab my bag for the next two weeks, I wave bye to my father, traveling up the steps and into the house as the scent of pine fills my nostrils. They said it would rain tonight, which sucks because we have a night run through the forest. Waving hi to a few people, I check in with a warrior of the pack, handing him my phone as he hands me my room key and number. Looking to the grand entrance of the house, my feet carry me across the polished wooden floor, up the wooden stairs, and onto the third floor as the carpet is now beneath my worn tennis shoes. As I get into my room, a smile spreads across my face to see a girl who I got along with quite nicely is going to be my roommate for these two weeks.

"Scared, excited, or regretting every coming?" Yvette asks, pulling her strawberry blond hair up into a bun. "Because I just want this week to be done and I'll be tanning in the Bahamas once this is done."

"I want to get it over with," I reply, placing my things upon the freshly made bed. The maids will clean the room for us while we train in the mornings. "I just don't see the point of this really. We take defense classes through our childhood and more when we finally shift. I don't get why this is necessary."

"Honestly, I see their reasoning, but we can defend for ourselves. It's not too common to run into a witch or vamp on campus because they don't really live in this country. Witches are for Europe and vampires for Canada or Russia." I nod in agreement, looking out the window to see people around and chatting. By the end of the night we will of hear all the rules and be on a run. For the past week I've gone on a run every morning before Augustus and I get together for the afternoon. He didn't like the idea of me being gone for so long but he wished for me to have fun with the aunt I will actually not be seeing.

In two hours the opening meeting is finished, the rules read, and no sight of Flynn as we are told to come to the north edge of the forest by subset. Only problem: there's a downpour of rain and no sun to be seen.

With my wolf itching to be let out and the time to go for a run, I leave my room, walking down the hall as I hear another door shut from the opposite end of the hall. It's the door for a more private room, one the size of a real bedroom. Looking around the corner for whoever came out of the set of double doors, my eyes widen to see him walking towards where I stand, his eyes locked on his phone. Of course he got to keep his, he's practically the Alpha of this little 'camp' for two weeks. I roll my eyes, heading for the stairs in hopes of Flynn to not catch me.

Just as I reach the first step, I freeze. "I have Alpha blood, Amory, not Omega," he comments right behind me, his tone holding no emotion. "I can smell you from blocks away. Nor am I dumb."

Turning my head, I look to Flynn as he runs a hand through his locks, those hunter green eyes locked on me. "I never said I was hiding."

"I never accused you of it," he points out, standing beside me as we look below to see pack members heading down. If people see me beside him, it will look innocent, for we have been seen as close friends for years now, it's only a matter of what he does to break those innocent ideas. "Two weeks without Augustus."

"Do you really have to be such a douche?" I snap, keeping my voice low as his lips pull into a smirk. "You have no place to interfere with my mate and I."

"I'm your Alpha."

"You're not his," I mutter, tilting my head to the side as I cross my arms. "I swear, Flynn, that if you think these two weeks have endless possibilities to try and get with me, you will be proven wrong completely over and over again." his lips form a straight line, mocking my stance as he too crosses his arms.

"You know I will try and try and try."

"Why? What's the point? I have a mate and I will not leave him."

Flynn shakes his head, looking to the entrance below as people file outside into the rain. "Because you don't give up on something or someone that you want, that you need. If you have a dream in mind, a career that you want, you try and try and try after every time you fail or are turned down because you are decimated, because you have emotion poured into this idea. This dream."

"I'm not a career," I add.

"It was a metaphors to how much I want you, Amory." He's said it flat out again. "I will not give up because I believe in us".

"There's no us, Flynn," I point out, watching as he lets out a sigh.

"There is an us, Amory."

I raise an eyebrow. "And how is that, Flynn?"

A ghost smile crosses his lips as my heart tugs a bit. "Because there is an us. Because you've helped me, you've let me drive you home, comfort you, even kiss you because there is a stronger bond than what you want to believe."

Looking away, I shake my head. "That's a lie."

"Look me in the eyes and say it."

I face the future Alpha, my eyes scanning his face as my heart clenches.

"You can't say it," he whispers, taking a step forward as I take one back.

"I made my choice. I picked Augustus."

Flynn shakes his head softly. "You picked Augustus? You picked him like you pick out a pebble in your shoe or pick a random card for a magic trick?" I scowl at his words. "You wanted him or you picked him like a random card...Amory, I lo-

"No." I walk away, heading down the stairs as I hear thunder in the background.

"Amory!" He snaps, following in pursuit as I rush out of the house and to the group of people my age, the rain instantly soaking me. I brush past people purposely, picking up their scents as I try and lose him a bit, the rain pouring down as the head warrior, Talon

Hastings tells us that it's a seven mile run through the mud and rain. As people begin to head for the trees to shift, I follow the crowd, trying to lose the future Alpha as I know what these next to weeks have in store: Flynn.

He will be everywhere. Hell, they should of even named this camp after him.

Camp Flynn: a living and breathing hell on earth.

Shifting behind a tree, I dig my paws into the mud, pushing off as I follow the crowd once more, knowing that these two weeks will be hard. Hard not because he will follow me and be around me constantly, but because of what he said. Because he dared me to look him in the eyes and tell him that what he said about us was all a lie. Because I could not bring myself to say it.

Why?

Because he's right, I picked Augustus like a stack of cards in a magic trick. But he's also wrong because Augustus was not some random trick, but my mate, and nothing is stronger than a mate bond. Not even gravity.

CHAPTER 15

My body is cold. My hair is sticking to my neck, soaked from the rain. My clothes are ruined, my feet making a squishing noise in the shoes I wear as the storm has passed and the run is finished. With my teeth chattering, I rub my arms, heading back into the massive pack house as I take off my shoes. I'm one of the last to come back, watching Flynn head back to the house before I would head back in. Looking to the grand staircase, I rather take a left, heading down the hallways as I know where the back staircase is located.

Wringing out my hair, I find the back staircase, climbing the two flights of stairs as I reach the third floor. The second I push open the door, my eyes go wide, hunter green eyes connecting with my own. I'm screwed.

"Avoiding someone?" Flynn asks, crossing his arms as he looks me over in my messy state. He has a mate out there. Let go now than let go later and only be hurt in return. This is a difficult situation because I have my mate and he has yet to have his. "After all, you've been running from me every time I get closer than fifty feet."

A lump forms in my throat, wondering what to reply with as he blocks my path. I want to change out of these damp clothes, to shower and get in clean clothes. Not here, facing Flynn as I know these next two weeks will only get worse every time he talks to me. "It's because of what I said earlier."

It's no question. He doesn't need the reassurance to know that he's right. We both know it's all about what he said earlier, how I picked Augustus like a stack of cards...but fate can be like that sometime. Fate can be a random occurrence and it happens so fast that you can question if you're swimming with the tide. But fate paired Augustus and I together, and sure some mates never happen because of massive reasons that shake your reality, but fate paired us and it is now taking action. I have suffered for so long that I now get what I have wanted. Sure, I wait. I waited because I could not fight. He was in love. Love. Flynn has someone out there who will love him for every fiber he is worth, and until then, he has to accept that.

"Flynn, it's best for the two of us if it's like this. It's best for me because Augustus is my mate and it's best for you because your mate is out there."

"Best for us?" Flynn asks, scoffing as he shakes his head. "You speak in the subject as if Augustus is some cure." I raise an eyebrow. "Best for us?! It implies that you feel something for me deep down and you know that going with it will hurt your heart. You think it will hurt your heart because you believe mates are a match made in heaven an will always work out in the end."

"Flynn-

"My parents are mates, Amory!" He snaps, taking a step forward as I feel caged in. "My father slept with other women and my mother forgives him every day. She tries to forgive him every day. Mates are not perfect and sometimes they don't work out."

"Your-

"My parents are not perfect an my father has confessed me that if he was not Alpha and my mother the Luna, he would reject her and move away."

I keep my mouth shut, knowing that Flynn has a point. I've seen mates tear each other apart and create a toxic environment before one leaves and never comes back. My uncle had that, how his mate left him. He said mates are made by fate, and sometimes, that feeling of overwhelming joy when your with your mate is only temporarily. He has fates brings you together, but it doesn't have to keep you together.

"Please hear me out."

"You know I made a choice. You know I picked Augustus."

Flynn shakes his head.

"You didn't make a choice. You followed the crowd believing that your mate is always your best pick," Flynn explains, his eyes searching my face for any sign of reaction to his words. His words that sting. His words that hurt because they are the truth. But fate...fate you are told stories of as a child for bedtime stories in this community rather than Cinderella or Jack and the Bean Stock. It's set in our society that you follow fate because it is always in your best interest. People who reject their mate are rare, usually frowned upon by the community even if their mate had to be rejected because of vampire or a rogue. You follow fate. You follow what society says. It's pathetic and weak, but the werewolf community is set on tradition. Hell, you break one traditional unwritten rule and you're seen as an imposter within the community. "Amory, mates are important, but sometimes, fate doesn't intend for a happily ever after."

He's right. But I don't want to admit it. My parents are mates, head over heels for one another. Yet again, Flynn's parents are mates and barely surviving to mask their true relationship to the pack. "I've waited for Augustus for so long," I whisper, my voice weak as I look over Flynn's shoulder, unable to look him in the eyes. "I didn't interfere with him and Molly because I knew he loved her. I respected that and let it happen because he deserved that happiness. But now him and Molly and done and I know he is happy."

Flynn shakes his head, running a hand through his thick locks of hair as I take in a deep breath. "I love him."

"What is love?"

"What?" I ask, rather confused.

"It's a simple question," Flynn explains, "What is love?" I don't know rather to give him some dictionary definition or try and search for one all on my own. "Because my mother once described it as being around that person and unable to hold back how much you love them. That love is where you will fight until you can no longer fight. Love is when you would die for the other person, where you watch them grow old with you, when you look forward to them being the first thing that you see when you wake up in the morning. Love is an endless amount of emotion." Flynn is passionate with how he talks, as if entering another dimension as I no longer recognize the boy before me. At school he's seen as someone to never turn your back on or even start a rumor about.

At school he'll punch a kid or turn down a girl without a second thought.

With me he is someone else. With me he has climbed through my window in the dead of night to pour out his heart to me over a girl. To me he will drive me home when he thinks I'm a danger to myself. To me he tries to get my wolf back, he fights for me to have my other half back that has four paws and fur. To me, he lets me see his family not as they are to everyone else, but who they truly are. To me...to me...to me...he lets me see the things no one else will ever get to see. To me...he trusts me and believes in me.

To me he needs me.

"Amory?" I blink, reminding myself where I am as I still stand wet, my hair a mess, my clothes wet with some mud, my shoes squeaky, and on full display to him in my worst appearance. "Mates may be made by fate, but fate only works to get them together, not to keep them together. Why do you think people can reject their mates?"

"I-I have to go. The week has just begun," I explain, pushing past Flynn as I head to my room, my vision creating a tunnel as everything else becomes a blur. My eyes are focused upon my door, Flynn all a blur as he catches up to me. It's too much. It's all too much to take in.

As I reach for the handle of my door, he takes ahold of my arm, spinning me around to meet those famous hunter green eyes so many girls say you could get lost in. A soft kiss is placed upon my lips, barely present as my heart skips a beat.

He pulls back, his lips inches from mine as his hot breath fans my cheek. "You're right, Amory," he begins, his voice soft as we hold a strong gaze. "The week has just begun."

CHAPTER 16

Monday. Monday is significant for two reasons: one being that it marks that I am halfway done with this camp, and two being that I have avoided Flynn for a week. Well, not really avoided, as I know he has given me space. I know he's tearing himself apart by giving me the space I need. But I'm not dumb for I know he will waltz his way back into my life sooner or later. After all, tonight we have a late game of capture the flag in human form. Through the thickest part of the forest will the game be underway, four teams, human form, and seen as a de-stress game for some fun.

I feel his eyes open me, how his presence fills the dinning hall the second he enters. As every other day, we all rise to our feet, letting him know that we do see him as our next Alpha, bowing our heads in respect as he enters. The second I hear his chair moving across the wooden floor, I can't help but look up today, and just as I expected, his eyes are glued to me. Blood rushes to my cheeks and I snap my head back down to the plate before me, reminding myself of my place. As he takes his seat, as do as well, the food ready to be eaten now as we dig in.

I don't eat, my stomach growling over and over as I stare at the egg, yogurt, and bacon before me. I am hungry, but my stomach tells me that I will throw it up the second I swallow it. Why? Because I'm nervous. Why? Because today he watches me. For the past week we have shared short glances, not staring at the other. After all, anyone with Alpha blood confessing something like that to a pack member is seen as a massive load. For someone with Alpha blood to be emotional before someone else shows great locality and respect. It shows a true friendship. A friendship that should not go further because I am chained to society and that I believe Augustus and I will not be like his parents or my uncle. We will not just reject one another. Then again, Augustus has no idea about my world or any aspect about it.

After breakfast, we head out for the day, the group that I am in following around two warriors as we practice defense in wolf form. Over the course of the afternoon, I catch glimpses of Flynn, watching as he leads groups or partakes in activities. He's good at this stuff. He's a good leader and protector. He will make a great Alpha one day, but I know his passion lies outside of the werewolf community and in a degree and job within the human realm. He seeks breakage from the society of tradition. Flynn believes that fate is just an option. Flynn believes fate is hard to ignore. He doesn't know what the mate bond is like, how every night I think of Augustus and what he is up to.

By night the sun is gone, my clothing now changed as I wear black running shorts and a black tank top, my sneakers on, hair pulled back right, and ready for a game. I'm on the yellow team, a yellow glow stick around my neck like the rest of my team as we stand on the western patch of the forest, our flag hidden in a tree stretching over a small creak. The leader of our group is a girl, Meghan Woods, a future warrior for the pack and one of Flynn's picks for his Delta. He already has his Beta picked for when he gets the Alpha title, and that boy, Cole, is on the green team. Meghan gives us our jobs, some people protecting the radius of the flag, and people like me chosen to be bait, and others to go and find the flag. Sure, bait sounds like a low blow, but I know to follow the orders.

As the dog whistle is blown by the head warrior, it piercing our ears shortly, letting us know the game has begun as we begin. The people set to find the other flags run out, some taking longer paths as others shorter ones. Meghan nods to my group, each of us heading out all alone into the forest to be bait as we take different paths from people actually after the other flags. I just hope to go back to bed without a broken limb as those are a bitch to heal.

I jump over a small steam of water, knowing some people finding the flags have taken the route of water to hide their scent. I also know I am being sent over to the blue team territory as bait where I know Flynn is directing the blue team. Hell, he's probably heading out to find a flag, making it safer for me to be in this territory without my nerves sky rocketing.

As I reach the blue team territory, I see them, faint glow sticks as I know a rule of the game is to keep your glow stick on at all times. Taking it off wouldn't help anyway because we have night vision thanks to being half wolf. Looking around, I take in the view before me, how the blue team members look like ants from the distance I am at, and as I'm about to charge over and surrender myself as bait for my teammates to get the flag, something seems off.

Just before I can move an inch to get the job done, my arm is grabbed, turning me around completely as I see him, his green eyes almost glowing in the darkness. Quickly he tears off my glow stick, throwing it into the ground as I see he doesn't wear his either.

"Not now," I snap. "We're playing a game."

"And you're bait and I've caught you, meaning you're out," Flynn refutes, offering me a cocky smile as he pulls me away from the territory the game is set upon.

"Please, Flynn, just drop it an-

His hand is over my mouth, keeping me silent as he interlocks his fingers with mine, pulling me deeper into the trees as I roll my eyes. "Amory," Flynn whispers as we come to a halt, turning around to face me as my heart clenches. "Hear me out."

"It's unfair," I whisper before he can say another word. "You're trying to terminate a relationship before it has really even begun. You're not even giving me a chance to see what Augustus and I can be." He shakes his head, pulling me closer as I take in a deep breath.

"Amory please listen to me."

"I have before, Flynn," I reply, my voice soft as I shake my head. "I've listened and know what you mean. I've listened and know that Augustus and I are mates and I need to see if we are a match."

"Amory-

"When did your feeling for me even start because four weeks ago you were taking Miranda home." Miranda, the raven-haired girl who watched him drive me home before their date.

"Prom." I raise an eyebrow. "Prom I realized the strong girl before me who loved her mate so much that she would not interfere with her mate because he was happy with someone else. I realized you were strong, kind, brave, and so much more." He pauses. "Miranda never made it to my house. I dropped her off after I did you, for I could not drop the emotion of hate for Augustus as I watched what he was putting you through."

I shake my head, my eyes tearing up. "I am with Augustus and I need to see if we are going to work."

"So you'll think about us?" Flynn asks, a ghost smile spreading across his face.

"I'll think about Augustus and I because he is who I am with."

Flynn's smile drops, his fingers once laced with mine now limp as he moves back. He's started to build a wall between us with my words. "Amory..." Flynn trails off, his voice weak as my heart clenches.

The whistle sounds, my body jumping at the sudden high-pitched noise. One team is out, their flag collected. But who? I watch the green team retreat, someone from the blue team placing the green flag in their stash as one team is done, two more to go. The yellow team and red team are next for the blue team. "Amory, please listen to what I have to say."

"You've said so much this week already, Flynn," I respond, back in away from the future Alpha as I know soon enough his pack members will be beside him and he will have to put on a strong character. "Just let this be how things are and not jump before reaching the obstacle."

"Amory, I lo-

"No," I snap.

Flynn grabs my arm, pulling me back to him as I meet his gaze. He's broken, his eyes tearing up as my heart falls to my feet. "Amory, I love you."

I get out of his grip, storming off to my team as I leave Flynn all alone in the woods. The whistle sounds agin, this time my team out as the blue team has captured out flag. Within another twenty minutes the red team I out and I watch Flynn being carried by his teammates as he holds up the four flags in victory. And so the party begins, the blue team celebrating as the others join in, but I head back to the pack house. Looking over my shoulder as I head back into the house, I meet his gaze, his smile softly fading as sadness fils those beautiful eyes.

Flynn loves me, and I cannot say anything back. I cannot say anything back because it is unfair to Augustus.

Heading up to bed, I leave the door unlocked for my roommate, sliding into the bed after changing back into an old shirt and sweats, closing my eyes as I know the night is over for me. I have one more week left and I need to survive, not be overwhelmed. I miss Augustus, I miss him holding me as we watch a movie or laugh as we look down upon old memories. Memories we created and remember because they made us realize how much we meant to the other. Some memories are bittersweet and some memories we laugh at because of how much we felt alive those nights.

Taking in a deep breath, I put in headphones to block out the noise of the party outside, kneeing it is for the best to keep my distance. I need to respect that and respect Augustus, for he trusts me to come back to him untainted and vice versa. Letting out a sigh, I prepare for the next week ahead, Augustus on my mind as I fade away into my sleep.

There's a small squeaking. Someone's moving around the room as my eyes shoot wide open. I turn on the lamp beside me, sitting up right away as I'm about to give him a piece of my mind.

"Listen here-

"Amory, you look like you've seen a ghost," Yvette, my roommate comments, taking a seat upon her bed. "The party is fun, everyone's having a good time."

"Why did you leave early?" I ask, settling back down in bed as she shrugs.

"Not my crowd really. I prefer adventures and late nights filled with that of the literary nature." I laugh, understanding what she means as I pull the covers tightly around my body to cocoon myself. "Besides, Flynn is being weird."

I raise an eyebrow. "How so?" I ask, looking out the window to see the future Alpha passing around a bottle of heavy liquor as a scowl crosses my face. "He's just going to get drunk like his friends are."

Yvette shakes her head. "I made small talk with him and he acted weird." I raise an eyebrow. "I've never seen anyone with Alpha blood be on the verge of tears." He's weak. He's broken. He wants me and knows he cannot have me. At least yet. Yet? "Weird, you would think he wouldn't dare disappear any emotion like that." I've seen him cry before.

"Believe me, people like him can get their heart broken," I mumble, switching off the light as Yvette nods in agreement.

"Still, she must be one hell of a girl."

CHAPTER 17

"Let me just say how grateful I am that you all came out here," Luna Willow announces as we all sit patiently during the closing ceremony as the last week has dragged on for ages. The night after the game, Flynn did not comes to breakfast, saying he was sick, but in reality: he had a hangover and didn't want to face me. In all honesty, I almost played sick that morning too. The week dragged on, barely seeing Flynn as he was trying to avoid me, not because he wanted to, but because he knew it was what I wanted. But now here I sit, dressed in a beautiful, mid-thigh length black dress, lace sleeves, a backless except for the thin layer of black lace, and my hair pulled back, my feet strapped into black heels and everyone else eager to begin the night. We have dressed up for the night, many other girls also in their signature black dress for a party as the boys wear a more formal suit, but not as much as they would for prom.

Flynn sits beside his father as his mother gives a short speech to those who attended, thanking us for our two weeks of the summer when we could be having bonfires or painting the town red. His eyes are on me every so often, his hair combed back yet a tad messy, his build nicely emphasized in his attire as a black tie is what makes me think of some shameful thoughts. Hell, all it would take is getting him alone and pulling him bye it-

Let's just say I've had a little to drink because of my nerves, knowing that this party will start off formal and the second the clock strikes twelve we will let loose. Alcohol is going to be passed around, music will be playing, my heels will replaced by flats, my hair down, and probably my body pressed against someone as I let loose and try to erase this night. I've heard about how these parties go, how some people let loose, some head to the woods for a hook up, others pass out drunk, and the wise head to bed before they have perhaps a tattoo of a toaster upon their left calf (last year's highlight story).

As the closing ceremony is done, we all rise to our feet, thanking the warriors who helped these weeks as well as the Luna and Alpha. Flynn leaves his parent's side, meeting up with Cole and Meghan as the pack house is left for our crazy events for the night. The Moon Goddess help this night not go up in flames as too many mistakes are made to count of ten pairs of hands.

Everything goes bye fast, for one second I'm in the pack house all collected, and the next my hair is down to my waist, my flats on, and letting loose as I take a shot of the alcohol before me. Yvette claps me on the back, taking one right after me as the future Beta, Cole, pours us another round. I take it, knowing my limits as I know how much I can take.

Soon I'm allowing the music to take over, letting go as I close my eyes, swaying to the music as I feel his eyes upon me. I need this night. Someone is behind me, I push away, keeping those eyes in mind as I want this night to myself. I need to forget the troubles of the night as I need to embrace the point of no return. No return because tomorrow I will wake up, knowing I can never redo tonight. No, I don't plan on sleeping with someone or streaking across the yard, but because I will go back to life tomorrow, with Augustus, and make Flynn suffer every time he watches us. I need to forget that tonight. I need to forget that soon Flynn will be heartbroken once more, but this, he cannot go to me for a haven, but only himself.

By the strike of midnight I've made myself tired than ever, swaying my body to the beat as Yvette is beside me, drunk and out of control as I am her anchor tonight. People have already snuck out into the woods to have some fun, others has gotten high, and others have forgotten their names. Tonight I am not Gatsby. Tonight I am Daisy, dancing through the night as I drink my alcohol as the one who plays Gatsby tonight watches me from the second floor. Every turn I make, every step I take, he watches with such intensity that it makes me take another shot. I am like Daisy, for I know the control I hold as well. I know the control I hold over Gatsby as I am in his domain, just out as reach as Tom is in my life, even if he's miles away. But this story is better. This time there is no Myrtle to interfere, only Daisy as Tom and Gatsby fight for her love. Fight like some award, but I know I am more than an award to both. I know I have them both head over heels, it's just a matter of which one has me in return.

With my hands running in my hair, I shut my eyes, raising my hands up to the sky as the bass drops and I find myself making my way away from the crowd and down a hall. My bare feet now walk across the wooden floor, the shadows of the hall enclosing around me as I let a ghost smile cross my lips as I take in the night. Stretching out my hands, I run my fingers across the cold walls, leaning back my head as I walk all alone on the hallway.

"Amory?" The smile stretches across my lips as I know where he is. "Amory." I walk forward, opening my eyes to see him before the massive window at the end of the hallway, the moonlight pouring in as he is now a silhouette.

I can smell the alcohol on his breath.

I can smell the sweat of the people from the dance floor.

I can hear the thumping of the beat and feel the vibrations of the music through the walls.

"Tell me something, Amory."

I stop in my steps, raising an eyebrow as Flynn walks forward, his thin black tie still on yet loose, his white shirt with the sleeves pulled up, his tan skin on display as I know that shirt hiss a well-worked body. After all, no one who has been with him keeps anyone from the details that he's got a great body. Hell, it doesn't taken 20/20 vision to know that.

"Tell me that you love only Augustus and no one else. Tell me that no one else holds a piece of your heart except Augustus and you'll never have to deal with me again." I know Flynn's alcohol limit, and I know he's drunk himself enough to drown in it. All because of me. All because I cannot be unfair to my mate.

"Amory?!"

I tilt my head to the side as he stands right before me, his fingers under my chin as I look up at him through my eyelashes.

"You know the answer," I whisper, leaning into his touch as I offer him a sly smile. "You don't need my answer to be sure in the matter." His eyebrows knit together as I know what he wants, what he wants to do so badly. "What's holding you back?" I pressure, winking as I watch his jaw clench.

"You." I await his full response. "You're holding me back." I pour my lips.

"Why would I?"

"Because you're drunk and so am I," he replies, removing his fingers as I let a frown form upon my face. "If we were in our right state of minds we would not be here. You would be telling me off and I would not dare take advantage of you because I could never do that to you."

I smile. "Your mate will love you."

He backs away. "I don't want a mate." I shake my head, knowing he has no idea what he is talking about. "I want you, Amory, because I love you more than anything and nothing you say can ever change that. No mate will just suddenly make me fall out of love with you because love is not that easy to forget, especially if I know you are who I should be mates with. Augustus should not of been picked as your mate, but me, because we are made for one another."

I shocked, one second in the middle of the hall and the next I'm against the wall, his body so close to be pressed against mine as his shadow looms over me in the pale moonlight. Tomorrow I already know what will happen, how I'll be back home, on a date with Augustus in the evening, back in his embrace, and Flynn heartbroken once more. Tomorrow we go back to our real lives and are no longer secluded from reality.

"What do you want from me, Amory?" Flynn asks, cupping my cheeks with his hands as a soft smile spreads across my face.

"The world."

"You won't remember a fraction of this night and neither will I...we will never remember tonight." He's right, we're both too drunk. I stumble trying to take hold of his hands, unable to keep my balance as I grab onto his tie, pulling him down with me as we fall to the floor.

He falls on top of me, a laugh escaping my lips as he does the same, his laugh filling the empty hall as my heart speeds up. My hands find their way to his chest, grabbing ahold of the expensive fabric as I bunch it up in my hands, pulling him closer onto me as he looks up. His eyes are full of surprise, searching my face for any sign of what will happen next as I know who waits for me back home.

I release his shirt, my arms wrapping around his neck as I pull him close, placing a kiss upon his lips, short and sweet as I close my eyes. Brief and I pull away, his eyes still closed as my heart races within my chest. I've screwed up. "Goodnight, Flynn," I whisper, his eyes opening as a new song begins. "Goodnight."

I'm gone, out of his grasp, out of reach, my bare feet upon the stairs soon rough as I climb the stairs. As I reach the third floor, I look below, now looking out upon the crowd below as the music plays. My eyes meet his in the mess, my heart stopping shortly as I know where this night must end: alone. Turning my back, I leave him, heading off to bed as I know Augustus awaits me, and we've held one another accountable, we trust one another, and I've broken that trust. I kissed Flynn on my own and know I have betrayed my mate.

I've given Flynn something he never needed, something I never wanted him to have. I've given Flynn something that he can use.

Hope.

I gave Flynn hope, and that is my first mistake.

Chapter 18

My bags are unloaded, my thair thrown up in a sloppy bun, my head pounding, and my sunglasses on to keep out the bright sun. It's like a scene from a movie about a dystopian society, how the rebel leaves and finds a new world that they are shocked by. I feel that way, how I've been gone for two weeks with no connections to the outside world and now I'm back. My phone feels as if it weights a ton, the wheel of the car unusual, and the smell of my mother's baking making me want to go ahead and get the freshman fifteen before college even starts.

"Amory!"

I smile, turning around as I am enveloped by his arms, a kiss placed upon my forehead as my heart warms up. Sparks fly everywhere, electrifying every fiber of my being as he spins me around. By the second I'm back on my own two feet, a slow and much-needed kiss is placed upon my lips, his hands on my waist, my arms around his neck. I've missed him. I've missed his laugh, his smile, his presence in general. Hell, my wolf is bouncing off the walls of my mind right now in joy.

"I've missed you," I greet, pulling away from the kiss as I meet his beautiful blue eyes. How I've missed looking into these eyes. How I've missed him. "What's the plan tonight anyway?"

Right when I got back home I got a text from Augustus informing me to dress up and be ready at six. He came back to welcome me here, four hours till our date. "A surprise," he whispers, looking to my gaze as my cheeks turn a pink color. "And wear a dress, not a nice shirt." I raise an eyebrow, wondering what exactly this date is that he has in mind. If anything, just being with my mate will be enough to keep me happy.

"I like the sound of that," I comment, releasing myself from his hold as I invite him into my house. With my parents instantly freeing Augustus like he's their son-in-law, the twenty minutes that he is here and chatting with them makes me feel content. My parents love him and so do I.

So do I. He's my mate after all, and I know he's not just some temporary love story that people will swoon over. This story is not heartbreaking where the reader cries and pities me, but where the reader smiles when they think of my future with my mate. My mate, my best friend, and my everything.

"See you soon," Augustus calls out as he heads to his car, waving bye as I do as well. As he drives off, I head back inside, a smile unable to erased from my face as my parents comment upon my mate in the dining room.

Within four hours I have my dress on, a pale peach dress that hits just below mid-thigh, a modest front, dip in the back, and emphasizes my best features as I pull on my nude wedges. Mother has pulled my hair back in a simple braid, a smile wide across my face as the clock strikes six. "Amory," mom begins as I sit beside her before my mirror. We sit in my room, making eye-contact through the mirror as I feel the atmosphere grow tense. "Mates a truly a wonderful thing to have. Your father and I love one another, but it's not the mate bond that did that. The bond brought us together and we simply fell in love." I raise an eyebrow as she takes a seat beside me, meeting my gaze without the mirror as my heart skips a beat. "Some mates don't understand that. Some mates don't understand that you can easily fall out of love."

Flynn. It's as if I'm talking to Flynn all over again.

"Amory?"

"Yes?" I ask, my throat running dry as the doorbell rings.

"Made a wise decision. Augustus is a great guy, but he is just a boy, he's not a god that can hand you the world on a gold plate. He's-

"He's human," I cut her off, taking in a deep breath. "And I love him."

She nods, helping me to my feet as we head for the door. As I reach the front door, I can sense him, I can sense that he is nervous. Once the door is pulled open, I'm shocked, a massive arrangement of flowers ranging in pinks to whites to yellows are before me tied with a beautiful pastel green bow. "Augustus," I gasp, taking ahold of the flowers to reveal his face, a smile plastered on his face with two dimples. His blond hair is neatly combed back, a simple pale-blue plaid, button-up shirt on, a nice pair of jeans, and his father's Camaro parked outside. He's ready for a beautiful date.

My mother takes the flowers from me after I thank him, mother putting them in a case as an arm wraps around my waist. Waving goodbye to my parents, we head out, Augustus opening the door for me as I slide into the car. "You went full out," I comment as he gets in, placing a soft kiss upon my lips as he hands me an envelope.

"You're mother told me that you love King Lear." Shakespeare. My favorite play and he got ticked to a Shakespearian company in the nearby city. "I figured you'd love to see it on our date."

"You were right," I reply, interlocking our fingers as the soft pure of the engine and his presence is all I need for a relaxing evening and amazing date.

Within four hours we are walking along the riverside, the brick path before us running along the local river as bridges cross over for people like us taking a late-night stroll. There are some couples walking as well, a few friends, and some families. Some people stop at local cafés for a small dessert or a drink, others take seats as they admire the city lights reflected in the water. It's beautiful tonight.

Augustus laughs as we talk about an old story from two years back when he was trying out for the football team. He never made it past tryouts, but he made his name stick with the coach even till graduation after he had fallen flat on his face after the first mile run, had an asthma attack, acted like it was nothing, and accidentally ate the wrong protein bar as he had an allergic reaction to the peanuts. Never the brightest kid of the school, but he was kind and loving, which made people adore him for who he was. Outspoken about being a klutz, smart, funny, and a sweetheart, he's the boy every girl wanted to take him and introduce to her parents. He's the boy I now take home and introduce to my parents not as my best friend, but as my boyfriend. Flynn is not the boy you take home and introduce to your parents, especially if you're human. Flynn is not who parents would really welcome with a warm smile. Yet mine did. Mine did because they see he is no harm.

"I never really wanted to try out," he explains, shaking his head as a soft smile crosses his face. "I tried out because my dad played for the school and I wanted to prove to him I could do something."

I laugh. "That landed you in the hospital," I point out as we take a seat at a table that overlooks the city. Skyscrapers rise high into the night sky, not a single song of our town as the bright lights outshine any sign of the small town. "I want to ask you a really weird question." Augustus nods, motioning for me to ask away. "Don't think me to be weird, but what do you think about the supernatural?"

He raises an eyebrow. "The show?" I shake my head. "The supernatural like vampires, fairies, and witches?" I wanted to add in my face, but I keep my mouth shut, just nodding my head for him to get on with his answer. "Sure, I mean, they're fun to scare people with for stories or Halloween, but they're just silly stories."

I nod, tilting my head to the side. "What about you?"

I think carefully about what I'm going to say. "We picture monsters in very different ways. Vampires for example, pale skin, sharp teeth, and red eyes. They were created long ago for stories, but you've also got to think we're they based off of a creature."

"You're implying that every monster created must of had some inspiration?" Augustus clarifies as I nod my head. "A werewolf is just a human and wolf creature. Vampires would have more background behind the creature, but werewolves are just some made-up creature that stuck with people."

If only he knew the irony of his words. All I would have to do is let my wolf take over and he would see a brown wolf before is very eyes replacing his girlfriend. It just takes one little blink of an eye.

"How about I ask you something now," Augustus changes the subject. He's not ready to know the truth yet. "What do you think about taking day off from town and heading to the beach?" It's a four hour drive. I would be with Augustus for four hours one way and going to the beach. "There's a group going from our class and I was wondering if you would want to go?"

I don't hesitate. "Of course!" He smiles, taking ahold of my hands as we fill the night with conversations about the future and the past. The past holds bitter memories and sweet memories. The future holds bitter memories and sweet memories. "Who is all going?"

"A group of about twenty," he informs, leaning back in his chair as I do the same. We look out upon the night, fingers interlocked, and with one another as it should be. "It's in three days."

"Count me in," I add.

Within ten minutes we are back to his car, Augustus helping me in as I kick off my heels for the night, blisters already present. Sometimes being a woman can suck ass. As Augustus hops in and pulls out of the parking garage, we hit a red light, and I take no time to waste as I pull him in for a short and soft kiss. The second the light turns green, I move back, Augustus driving off as a small smile spreads across his face.

"You're perfect, Amory," he whispers. "You're sweet, caring, kind, independent, trusting, loyal, funn-

"And you are perfect too, Augustus," I say, tilting my head to the side.

"Every time I touch you, it feels as if my heart is about to break out of my chest and my body feels alive." The mate bond. I cannot tell him yet, but soon he will know. Soon he will meet my wolf and we will face hardships. "Please tell me you feel something like that."

I nod. "Any simple touch results in sparks as cliché as it sounds."

He nods, briefly looking my way as we drive on the silent highway. "I felt dead without you in town for the last two weeks. It was eating me alive every night to know I had no way to contact you."

I lied. I had lied and I feel only guilt right now. Guilt not because I cannot tell him where I was, but also because Flynn kissed me. And I kissed him.

I cannot keep steady around these two. I cannot keep my head on straight around these two. Augustus is my best friend and mate....and what is Flynn to me? Who is Flynn to me? No, he's not some attention or random person I hang around. No, he's not just in my life because he's the Alpha or the heartthrob of the school. He's around me because....because I don't know. Every second I'm in my car, I think of him, how he watches the road ahead, how he taps his fingers to a song, how he sings the chorus and smiles. Every time I'm in the pack house, I think of him. Every time I'm in my room, I think of him, how he will confess his heartbreak to me and I will comfort him. He cannot leave my mind. Those hunter green eyes have cursed me.

Have damned me to the point of no return.

As we pull before my house and Augustus kisses me goodnight, I watch as Augustus drives away. A piece of me wishes it was not Augustus that had taken me out, but a boy with green eyes.

Chapter 19

y whole body is frozen, my fingers shaking is the only
movement I can seem to create, my heart pounding in my
chest as if it might explode, and my eyes locked on the silhouette.
The wolf runs across the forest floor, the darkness of the forest
making it a perfect night for a hunt for the wolf, his gigantic body
not creating a single sound as his paws hit the forest floor as he
chases his prey. He's the perfect hunter, imposing and silent as he
strikes his prey. And he gets his prey, tackling the fellow wolf as his
practice is cut short, after all, he saw me pull in near the path only
two minutes ago. I have simply watched, having a feeling settle in
my stomach that he is not the type of wolf you want to hunt you
down, for you would be the prey stuck in the big, bad forest as he
hunts you down. There's no way he can lose you...he was trained
to be the best.

Second best until his sister met a painful end to her life that sent
his family spiraling down into a mess.

As for me, I can barely even catch a rabbit, less try and train the
way that he does nonstop because his father holds standards for

him. Standards that push him until he breaks every fiber of his being and is yelled at until he heals up and begins again.

That's why he will soon be called Alpha. That's why he does not want the title.

He shifts behind a tree, coming out soon with a pair of sweats hanging low on his hips as my eyes stay locked with his.

He takes in my attire, the dress, the heels, my hair curled as I have let it down, and my lipstick needing to be reapplied. The second Augustus dropped me off I stood in my driveway, contemplating the whole night over and over. Augustus gave me his world, a piece of it that he had planned out. Augustus made me laugh, he made me smile, and he made me feel the sparks.

Augustus made me feel the sparks of the mate bond and I dug my grave deeper. I remember where he took Molly on dates, how they would go to a meal, go to a fair, the beach, or just simply sit in his car and watch the sunset. Augustus would pour out his heart to me about how much he was head over heels and wanted to even marry her.

Augustus was in love with her and now, as he looks into my eyes, I could tell tonight that it was not over. He ended it with Molly all because of one kiss where the mate bond occurred. All it took was one kiss and he was hooked, hooked not because he wants me for me, but because he wants me for the way he feels around me. Being around your mate makes you feel alive and as happy as ever...that's all we have felt. My mother and Flynn are right, the mate bond brings you together, but it's not superglue, it's simply a glue stick that is temporary and easy to pull apart.

"Amory?" Flynn asks, running a hand through his locks as I find myself taking in a deep breath. "How was your date?" He looks broken as he says those words.

I open my mouth, wanting words to escape, but the silence fills the gap between us. My car lights are still on, illuminating his face as his sharp features are present and his hunter green eyes seem to flow and appear as bright as stars.

"I-I..." I trail off, shaking my head as I let out a groan of frustration. Running my hands through my hand over and over, I form knots, my fingers stuck as I close my eyes. Flynn respects my state of mind, simply waiting patiently as I take in a deep breath. Looking up, I open my eyes, locking with his soft gaze as my heart flutters. "Superglue."

"What?"

"Superglue and a glue stick. Love is superglue and the mate bond is a glue stick."

He crosses his arms, cocking his head to the side. "Did the date go so bad that you got drunk?" I scowl, shaking my head as I find my courage, taking ahold of his hands with my own, causing Flynn to raise an eyebrow.

"The mate bond helps bring people together, but it's not strong. Easily the two mates can fall out of love as they slowly pull apart. Love is like superglue, a death sentence to get your heart involved in just like if you glue your fingers together with. Pulling away those fingers glued with superglue fucking hurts and takes time to heal, but the mate bond easily comes apart."

"A...weird analogy," he comments, surprised as I take a step forward. "What is this about?"

"I-

"Flynn!" The Alpha tone is strong, my head instantly bowing as Flynn looks to his father. "Why are you not training?"

"I finished for the night," he replies. He is done, hell, if my parents were doing this to me, I would of been done at seven in the evening, not four in the morning. "Amory drove over for a chat."

I peek from under my eyelashes, looking as the tall Alpha strides over in a few steps, arms crossed, eyes dark in the moonlight, and the atmosphere turning tense. "If you finished your training, you go home, not let her get in the way." Disrespect. I hold my tongue, not wanting to speak up for myself and risk my safety and reputation in the pack. "Go, Amory."

Looking up to the Alpha, I switch my gaze to Flynn, his jaw clenched, eyebrows furrowed together. He's pissed. With his eyes he seems to be telling me to stay, to stay for him and speak up for myself. But I cannot disrespect my Alpha. But I cannot give up on this. This? Wanting to be with a male who has a mate awaiting him while I have a mate as well. I love Augustus because of the mate bond and not because I truly love him. Sure, we are best friends, but nothing more, and now I have a chance at ruining that relationship. Flynn does not believe in mates, letting me know that he won't fall head over heels for his mate, but he has no idea what he's saying. Mates are impossible to just shake off.

"She's staying until she wants to leave," Flynn snaps, his Alpha tone present as my eyes widen. He's just dig his grave.

"Excuse me," the Alpha growls, charging to his son as Flynn lets go of my hands.

I watch as the first punch is thrown, Flynn's head jerking to the side as my heart stops and everything happens slowly. I watch as the Alpha grabs his son by the arm, landing another punch, Flynn's lip busted as his jaw is red. I scream as I watch the Alpha land one last blow upon his son, right to his nose as I hear a crack.

Then everything happens so quickly. One second Flynn is standing and the next he's on the ground, his father telling me to 'aid his son like the fixer upper I am when it comes to his family,' and the Alpha shifting as he head off into the night.

I'm shocked, speechless as I see Flynn, on his knees, in pain as blood pours from his lip and his nose is broken. I'm in pain just looking at him.

"Flynn!"

I run over, grabbing ahold of his shoulders before he can fall over, pulling him into my arms. I run my hands through his hair, trying to calm him down as I know his wolf wants to surface. I've never seen that. I've never seen Flynn be beat like that and left to suffer all on his own. How does Luna Willow even put up with this?

"Hey, let's go. I'll take you to my place," I whisper, wrapping my arms around his neck, feeling his heartbeat increase like crazy. He's in pain. He's in so much pain not only physically but also mentally. "Flynn?"

Pulling back, I meet his eyes, brimming with tears as my heart breaks for him. His lip is busted open, blood running down his chin, his jaw already turning black, and his nose horrible to look at. He did this all because of me. He did this because his father was disrespecting me and him. How? Why? Why would he do this for a girl that pushes him away for her mate although she knows who she wants? Superglue.

"Come on," I whisper, placing a soft kiss onto his cheek, helping him to his feet. With an arm around his waist, I lead him to my car, helping him into the passenger's side. Getting in, I pull out of my parking space, turning on the radio as a small smile crosses his face with the song that plays. It's a song I've watched him bang his head to and sing along with. He hums to the tone to keep himself calm as I drive, the road lit by my lights as I try and get back fast.

As we pull into my driveway, I turn off the car, unbuckling as I lean back in the seat. Turning my head, I meet his gentle gaze. "Why?"

"Why what?" Flynn asks, trying not to move his mouth too much as the blood is starting to dry up.

"Why do that? Why stand up to him if you knew what he would do?"

He shakes his head, getting out of the car as I let out a deep sigh. Hopping out, I help him to the front door, telling him to stay silent as we enter. By the time we're in my room, I sit him down on my desk's chair, rushing into my bathroom to grab medical supplies. Grabbing bandages, paper towels, water, and other items, I enter my room, Flynn holding a picture frame in his hand. I know that picture from last summer, when I went with him and some friends to the beach. It was a good day, one that made me realize how good of a guy he could be more than a heartbreaker. "Ready?" I ask, grabbing his attention.

Taking a seat beside him, I help clean up the blood, helping his lip as I know it will be healed within the next hour. As for his nose, we both know what I have to do.

"Ready?" I ask, positioning my fingers as his eyes go wide.

"No," he states, fear in his tone as a soft smile plays across my lips. "Why did you allow yourself to get beat up all because you stood up for yourself and me?" I ask again, pressing my fingers gently upon his nose.

"Just do it."

I nod, pressing sharply as the cracking of cartilage can be heard. I cringe, pulling back as Flynn throws his head back in pain. "Goddess, Goddess that hurt," he says, grinding his teeth as I quickly shove some tissues to his nose, helping with the blood as he looks back to me.

He smiles and I raise an eyebrow.

"Superglue."

"What?" I ask, getting to my feet as I clean my hands.

"You asked me why I did what I did." I nod. "Superglue."

Chapter 20

It's bright outside already, the sun burning my eyes the second they squint open. Immediately I turn my head, pushing it into the pillow as I take in a deep breath. I can smell food already downstairs, probably cold by now, but at least I know there's something to eat this morning after such a long night. I blindly reach for my phone, my hand searching my bed as it does a wiping motion, the cold device soon in my hands as I unlock the piece of technology. Two texts from Augustus.

Augustus.

Rolling onto my back, I hit a warm body, my eyes widening as I yelp, jerking away to find Flynn still fast asleep. I forgot that I had offered him a spot on the bed last night after I didn't want to send him home, fearing that only more drama would occur. He offered to sleep downstairs for me to only explain how my parents would wake up confused to find their future Alpha asleep on their living room sofa. After all, he's stayed here overnight before, right beside me as I slept because he was broken.

Pushing myself up and onto my elbows, I take a look at the future Alpha before me, how his dark locks frame his face, messy from a rough night. His jawline is strong, his cheekbones high, eyebrows enough that any girl would kill for, and his eyelashes long. The only off-setting things about him are the bruised jaw covered in black and purple, the nose all red and black, and his lip where the area is fully healed now. To think his father did this to him just because he could not control himself. To think a father would be willing to land a hand like that upon their son. It makes me sick.

Flynn has his sweats on still, but he wears an oversized t-shirt of mine from a tennis camp where I failed miserably. He sleeps like a brick. Goddess help him, I could of mistaken him as dead a couple of times.

"A picture will last longer," he mumbles, his voice hoarse from just waking up as my eyes widen. "Do you have Advil?" I nod, getting out of bed as my feet hit the cold floor. Grabbing the pill from my bathroom cabinet, I also grab him a water bottle, looking around the doorway to see him sitting up. He stretches, the shirt not hiding the fact that you can tell he's built, all the years of swimming paying off.

"Here," I announce, walking around to where he sits up, handing him the bottle and pill to help release his pain.

I decide to take the seat beside him, pointing my toes as I become nervous. I don't know what to do now. Augustus texted me asking about another date tonight, yet I know what I want now. I know who I want now. I know that I cannot do this, I cannot be unfair. I cannot go on a date with someone I do not love when there's a boy beside me who I love and he does as well. It's unfair to Augustus and to Flynn, but Flynn has a mate just waiting for him. Any day now she could walk into his life and he could never spare me a glance ever again.

"Are you going home today?" I ask, my voice soft as he runs his thumb over his bottom lip, checking that the wound is fully healed.

"Have to." I raise an eyebrow. "My mother plans on her and me to approach my father today about college."

"Can you postpone it?" I ask, worried about him as he will be approaching his mother upon a delicate topic.

He shakes his head. "I cannot. I have to be brace not only for myself, but my mother as well." I know what he means. I understand him, but I don't want him to go there expecting a battle to only result in a war by the time it's over with. "I'll call you and tell you how it goes."

"When are you going to do it?" I ask, getting to my feet as Flynn does as well. He shrugs, reaching for his phone, checking the time as I can hear the garage door open.

"I need to head out, I've got ten minutes to get there." I nod, knowing Flynn is distant. Distant because he's scared. The big and bad wolf is scared and I don't blame him. Can future Alphas not be afraid? What law determines that? None.

As he opens the window to sneak out, I find myself biting my lip, wishing he didn't have to go.

"Almost forgot," he informs, turning back to me as I grow curious by what he means.

I'm pulled forward, a hand on my hip and the other upon my cheek, a short yet passionate kiss pressed against my lips as I'm shocked. From how he woke up, I never expected him to do this. As he pulls away, my eyes are wide, a smirk on his face, and before

I know it, he's gone, running through the backyard as he shifts, his clothes tearing and a wolf replacing him.

Damnit, I actually liked that shirt.

<><>

In three hours I'm getting into my car, an extra pair of clothes packed, my hair pulled back, and putting on my playlist as I pull out. I plan on going for a run, but no where close to where the Alpha typically goes for one, but one rather on the outskirts of town on the Eastern side. No one runs out there because the ground is not damp, the trees are too many, and there's hardly any sunlight.

The drive soon comes to an end, my car parked as I hide my keys under a tire. With my figure hidden by a tree, I undress, shifting quickly into my brown wolf as I ruffle my fur. Right away I pounce, my paws digging into the ground as I shoot off through the woods, jumping over logs and avoiding tree trunks. The wind is strong as it blows my fur, my wolf having the time of her life as we do around four miles.

My mind is clouded with questions, questions upon how Flynn is doing. Last time he had that chat, I was there, and I believe I was one of the reasons his father did not overreact like he did last night. His father makes me sick. He cheats upon his wife, Luna, and mate, and then beats his son.

I slow down my pace, a light jog now what I do as I think of what I will have to tell Augustus. Am I going to reject him? I owe him that, yet rejecting him would reveal the truth. If I break up with him this soon in the relationship and say some weird shit about mates, he's gonna flip and think me be crazy, demanding an explanation. If I break up with him and don't reject him, it's doing him no justice as the mate bond will still be present. He deserves to be rejected if we end it because then he would not have that feeling of sparks every time he touches me. He would not feel things for me that are no longer worth while and vice versa.

As I get back to my car, I get ready to shift, only for my wolf to be curious yet worried as the future Alpha leans against my car, his sleek one parked right next to mine. What is he going here? How did the chat go? I shift behind a tree, putting on my clothes before I go to meet him. Once done, I walk towards him, only to stand still as he takes few strides to reach me.

Suddenly it all happens so fast, how he wraps his arms around me and pulls me tight against him, his lips locked with mine. My eyes close, arms wrapping around his neck as they eventually land in his hair, tangled in the locks as he only holds me tighter. The second me need to breathe, he pulls away, yet still holds me close, as if me close is the only cure to what is going on.

"Just talk when you're ready," I whisper, rubbing his back as I feel him shake, his face buried in the crook of my neck. His lips tremble against my skin, his eyelashes becoming damp as they brush against my skin. Something happened and I don't think I'll ever be able to forgive the Alpha. I hold the future Alpha in my arms, telling him he doesn't have to talk, to just not hold back anymore. I've seen him cry before, but barely much. Emotions are hard to see from this male, but for me, he doesn't hold back.

"Amory," he whispers, taking in a shaky deep breath. "Can we get out of here? Just run away for a few days? Go somewhere as do something?"

He's wanting to run from his problems just as I was doing weeks ago and still am.

"Why? Where will that get you? A short break from reality? You will only return weaker because you know running will let you escape for a little," I explain, trying to not speak too loud, his hold loosening up. Soon, he pulls away, his eyes red as he nods his head. "Flynn, I am here for you."

"I know." He pauses briefly. "But my father can never understand." I nod, letting him know I am here for him. "He told me that dreams are just all shit. He told me that we do not get to pick when the Alpha title awaits us. He said Alphas do not get to chose their destiny, but that they must follow the path of an Alpha and all of this shit." He's keeping me from something else. "He said I could either be here for the pack or I can come back. He said the second I change majors, I've secured my fate."

My eyes widen and hate fills my every fiber. How dare the Alpha say this!? How dare he think his son to be some puppet or being without free will. How dare he make Flynn suffer this when all Flynn has ever done is try to show him how vital he can be. He pushes limits beyond compare to impress his father and earn his respect, not to be told he could be made rogue and disowned. But tradition is everything. Every individual with Alpha blood next in line for the title takes the title. Take the title or...or you're done for. For his father to threaten him with this massive of an issue, it truly shows his father's respect.

"Let's just get away for a day," he whispers, taking my hand as he pulls me back to our cars. "One day just to relax."

I nod, thinking about what could all happen. "Where?" I ask, finding myself placed upon the hood of his Porsche, Flynn beside me.

"Anywhere," he replies. "Let's just drive somewhere for the day."

Flynn needs this. He needs a break from all of this, everything with his father. "Fine. I'm up for it," I announce, looking up at the sky as Flynn nods his head, turning to face me as I close my eyes. "Just don't get us lost." Looking back to Flynn, he nods.

I watch as he smiles, one that makes me forget about the bruise on his jaw and the red nose of his. But my heart drops to my stomach, reminding myself about a girl that awaits him. His mate. His mate that fate wants him to be with, to feel the mate bond. The mate bond blinded me and I saw that even if later on, but will he be able to see it? Will he forget everything he has told me and push away logic.

"What?" He asks, raising an eyebrow as I look away, to my car. Augustus never got a text back from me. Augustus will soon have to learn that I can no longer be part of our relationship. "Amory?"

"You have a mate out there," I whisper, my voice cracking as he shakes his head. "You have a mate out there and she will be the best girl you'll ever see. You'll go head over heels for her and-

"Stop."

"Flynn-

"Amory, I know what you're worried about," Flynn interrupts. "I know. I know." He runs a hand through his hair. "Do you trust me?"

Do I trust him? Do I even have to question myself?

"Yes, I trust you."

He nods. "Then do not worry."

CHAPTER 21

Courage. It's a tricky thing. It takes courage to do things and sometimes, you would rather play the coward. I know right now that I would rather play the coward, rather just cut off contact than speak face to face. But life is hard and if you play the coward, it is not only unfair to the other party, but also to yourself. So here I stand, at the front door of his house, my palms sweaty, my nervous all bundled up and ready to combust, and my mind running through a million different possibilities. Three knocks and my hands return by my sides, listening for any movement on the other side.

"Amory?" He asks, confused as I stand before him, the early morning bright, and I've just come from a long jog that helped me calm down a bit. "We're you in the area?" He just woke up from what I can tell, his hair all messy, face unwashed, and clothes wrinkled from a deep sleep.

I take in a deep breath. "I was sort of in the area," I reply to his last question. Meeting his blue eyes, I pull myself together. "We need to talk and I'm sorry I woke you up." He can tell by the serious tone of my voice that this is important, how he comes from relax to attentive in a mere second. Nodding, Augustus opens the door to his house wider, allowing me into the homey house as he shuts the door behind me.

"What's up?"

Courage. Don't be unfair. It's unfair anyway, how I was with him while I was slowly seeing that it's not him I want, but a boy who has a girl out there just waiting to meet him.

"I know how this happened all really quickly..." I begin, watching as he awaits my words. "But I have to call us off. Whatever we are, I have to call it off."

"What!?"

"I'm breaking up with you," I whisper, my heart feeling as if it's been stabbed. How will rejection feel anyway? Worse? Most certainly it will, there's no denying it. "I'm breaking up with you because I think it is best."

"On what grounds?" He asks, his voice stern as my throat runs dry.

Do I tell him that I've fallen head over heels for another while I was with him? Do I tell him we happened to quick and he is probably still in love with Molly? Hell, he broke Molly's heart, yet I believe that he will go back to her because he still loves her. You cannot fall out of love just because of one kiss. "On the grounds that I-I think that I love someone."

"Someone like who? How did this happen? When? Was this going on the whole time?" He asks, enraged as my wolf cowers. Our mate is mad at us and the mate bond is still present. "Was this going on from the second I asked you out, because if so, that's a very low blow."

"I know," I whisper. "I just realized it days ago, but I thought I could push him away, but I can't, Augustus. I can't because he's won me over and I feel like a jerk for doing that to you. I thought that I could forget my feeling for him, but I can't."

"So our date, was that you trying to think you could forget your feelings for him?"

Silence.

He's broken.

But that's the mate bond. I know he's not broken and that if the mate bond was not present, he would be fine. How do I know this? Because he was never in love with me, but with the thought of me. We were both in love with the thought of one another because that's what the mate bond does: it's a glue stick.

"Who?"

"Why?" I ask, my eyes beginning to water as I see his lips form a thin line.

"Because I'm going to beat the son of a bitch to a pulp."

I shake my head. "I am ending this relationship because it is unfair to the two of us, unfair to you because I have feeling for someone-

I'm cut off, Augustus pulling me in for a passionate and aggressive kiss, as if reassurance for him as the sparks fly. The sparks are just a side effect that does nothing. The sparks are a glue stick and they are temporary for us. I push him away, taking a step back as I see his jaw clench. "I love you, Amory."

I shake my head. "You love Molly."

He's speechless, watching as I walk to the front door, opening it and shutting it as I head to the sidewalk. I did it. I broke up, but I have to reject him. I have to reject him because he cannot go around still having a connection to me when it really means nothing. Molly is who he loves and I know that cannot change. Molly deserves him because she too loves him. I take off, jogging around the corner as I leave Augustus alone, my heart beating painfully in my chest as a tear falls down my face. I wipe it away quickly, increasing my speed as I have to get away. Today I was brave by actually letting Augustus know that I had feeling for someone else. If this had happened a month ago, I would of simply told me him were over and would of never told him the reason why. I owe it to Flynn, to how he stood up for his father not only for himself, but for me. I stood up for us today as well, ending the relationship with my mate as it was unjust. Ten points to Gryffindor just now.

Arriving home, I see the car parked outside my house, the sleek car making my own look like a scrap of tin on the side of the road. He's not in his car, and by the looks of it, my parents have let him in and I just pray that they are not making a big deal out of the Alpha's son being here. Jogging up the steps, I pull out my keys, opening the door to hear laughter followed by a snort from my mother. Piercing around the corner and into the kitchen, Flynn sits at the breakfast bar, cracking a joke to my mother who pours him some ice water.

"Oh, Amory," mother greets, a massive smile upon her face. "Flynn just came over for a visit."

"A visit?" I ask, looking to see a plate of bacon and scrambled eggs before him as a fork is in his hand. "Breakfast?"

"Come and make yourself some," she replies. I frown as she made Flynn breakfast and not me.

"Why are you here?" I ask Flynn, looking the clock to see its barely even eight. "Up early? Bored?"

"Both." I nod, heading to the fridge as I grab a water bottle.

"I'm going to head to my room, I have some college documents to take care of," I lie, needing privacy right now as I want to burry my face in my pillow and sob. It's pathetic, but the mate bond is strong. "Nice to see you, Flynn."

My mother watches me as I head up to my room, closing the door behind me as I don't bother to lock it. I know he's going to try and get in here anyway. He always finds a way. I can hear them downstairs, wrapping up their conversation as I plant myself into my bed, the covers thrown over my body as I enclose my body in the sheets. My hands fly to my mouth, muffling the sobs that follow as my eyes are filled with tears. I did this all because I love someone else. I did this and have yet to reject him.

I can hear the footsteps, how he gets closer every second. I now wish I should of locked my door, to at least felt him by two minutes and collect myself. Rolling onto my stomach, I close my eyes, my eyelashes wet as they brush against my pillow. The door opens, his scent strong as he enters the room, striding in as if he owns the place, but I know he's here because he knows I'm in a bad state with now.

"Amory?"

I pull the covers down a tad, bunching the ends just below my nose to hide my trembling lips as I want to sob again.

"Amory."

He quickly walks over, his hands resting up my cheeks, wiping away the loose tears as I shake my head. "I thought rejection would feel like this, not just breaking up," I whisper, my voice cracking as Flynn nods his head, his eyes filled with sadness. He's hurting because I am too. Flynn crouches down to his knees, eye level with me as he rests his chin upon the bed. "I told him that we loved the idea of us together, not each other." Flynn nods, his face glum as I take in a shaky breath. "He looked heartbroken, but it was just the mate bond."

"How about you?" He asks as I roll my eyes. "I'm sorry, that was dumb to ask-

"My state is pretty well explained by my posture right now," I mutter, closing my eyes as I try and calm down my breathing. I need to calm down. I need to relax and try to not remain in the same state. I wonder what Augustus is doing? I wonder if he's like me, all depressed and miserable as he feels broken. I haven't even rejected him yet.

"Amory?"

"What?" I ask softly, trying to keep my emotions at bay.

"You're strong." I open my eyes. "You have courage and did not leave Augustus to an unfair or unjust breakup. You showed strength today and traits that many do not have the courage to display."

"To break up with someone?" I scoff.

"To tell someone that you love someone else and so do they," I mutter, turning onto my side to face Flynn. "I told him I loved the idea of him but not him. I told him he still loves Molly."

"Amory," Flynn whispers, tucking a strand of my messy hair behind one ear. "I want you to know-

"That what you're proud of me? You're proud that I broke up with someone?" I snap, instantly regretting my words as I shake my head. "I'm sorry, Flynn, I-I just had such a chaotic morning and you don't deserve this treatment," I apologize as I scan his face, his jaw lightly bruised as his nose is a tad crooked. He's back to normal for the most part. But what is normal for him? Daily beatings by his father and told he could be disowned and never be taken back into the pack? His father is miserable and I pity Alpha Cade.

"You don't have to apologize," Flynn whispers. "I feel responsible for this."

I shake my head. "It was my call. I called the shots. You did nothing," I explain, inching forward to where he is before my bed. "Can you promise me something?"

Flynn nods.

"You may not like what I have to say," I warn, my eyes scanning his own for any sign of resentment.

"Say it."

My heart skips a beat.

"Promise me that you'll tell me when you find her."

He knows exactly what I mean. He knows exactly who we are speaking of and he knows what kind of load his promise could put upon me. Him telling me when he's found his mate means that he will be there was my heart is broken and I wonder if he will break up with me right away.

"Am-

"Promise me?"

Flynn looks torn, knowing the emotional damage that could cause. His eyes search my face, his hands cupping my tear-dried face as he wonders what to say. He knows he will have to drop that load when the time comes and watch as I break apart.

"I promise."

Chapter 22

I pull the brush through one last time, setting it down upon the counter as I look up at the girl before me. The girl who sulked the whole day in bed yesterday as Flynn respected my privacy. But today I head out, the sun not even out yet as Flynn is about to drop by and pick me up. Today we head out to escape the world and I pray we do not get lost. Not lost in location as our phones cannot gps us back to society, but so lost in our emotions that we forget what lies ahead for us. College and the chance of Flynn being rejected by his father. So lost in our emotions that we forget about the reality of his mate. I do not know who she is or when she will appear, but I do know there's a chance that she could tear us apart. I believe in Flynn and his strength on how the mate bond does not mean you are in love, but I worry that he only says it because he has not experienced the bond yet.

I can hear the car pull up, the sound of the engine turning off. I pick up my bag, heading for the front door as the lights are all off within the house and my parents asleep. They trust Flynn with my life. Not because he is the future Alpha, but because he is loyal and cares for me. Locking the door behind me, I turn around to face the car, a Jeep replacing what is usually a sleek car. Flynn stands by the passenger side, opening the door for me as a smile crosses my lips. The moment his eyes meet mine, my heart speeds up and I find my life going by fast as I'm soon in the car, Flynn taking the wheel.

"So where is our destination?"

He smiles.

"What all did you pack?" He asks, taking a left onto the freeway as I see we are headed east. "What types of shoes?"

"Sandals and sneakers. Didn't know which I would be needing," I respond, looking back to the small duffle bag. "My mother hinted at sun screen and a swimming suit just to be prepared. I'm guessing that you told her."

"Gold star to Amory," he comments, plastering his pearly whites across his face. "To the beach for a day of getting away." I wait for his next words. "Your mother made sure I would tell her."

"Well, I can't wait to see where this day takes us," I announce, plastering my own smile across my face as he turns up the classic rock. For the most part, I look out the window, humming the chorus as Flynn takes the guitar solo, mocking the sounds as the ride is not filled with awkward silence. Awkward silence like when I think of how I am to reject Augustus. I could reject him while we are drunk, for him to not remember. But what justice could be done there?

"Flynn," I announce, his response is turning down the music as he awaits my words. "What..." Asking the question would lead to an argument that I do not want to ruin this day. "Did you bring sunscreen?" He raises an eyebrow, nodding his head as I have gotten away with an argument. But how will I reject Augustus? Just pop out of no where and explain to him that I'm a werewolf, a thing of fiction, and we are mates and I am rejecting him. Yah, because that will work out just peachy.

As the ride comes to any end, we find ourselves parked between two trucks, the ocean before us as my heart skips a beat. It's been two years since I was here. I've missed the smell and the sand. Looking around, I see waves crashing upon the shore, chairs and umbrellas set up, a few beach bars, and friends having fun. There's a ton of people our age here today.

Augustus.

He asked me about going to the beach.

This is the group from our school.

I take a closer look, recognizing a girl with scarlet hair, the boy with her. These are my classmates and fellow pack members even. These are the people Augustus was going with. Is going with. He's here. He's somewhere. But he's here. "Did you know these people would be here?" I ask, wondering if he knew about this group.

"No clue," Flynn replies, turning off the engine as he heads for the trunk where a surfboard is stored away. "Do you want to change in here? The windows are tinted." I nod, grabbing my bag as Flynn shuts the doors, isolating me as I take in a deep breath. Augustus will see me where with Flynn and drama will be the result.

I change quickly, a navy bikini top on that I've now covered with my shirt, my bottoms on as well as they are covered by my shorts. Hopping out, I see Flynn leaning against the car, waiting for me. We head out, Flynn taking my hand as he pulls me close.

Augustus said that he would beat whoever stole me from him to a pulp. Flynn is the one who stole me. Augustus could never beat

Flynn to a pulp, it would be the other way around. I'm worried. I'm scared.

We wave to a couple of people from school as we head to the beach to pitch camp for the day. With an umbrella set up and towels laid out, we have set up shop, laying down as I put sunscreen upon my body, not wanting to burn. "So what do you think about playing soccer with a group from school?" Flynn asks, motioning over to a group of ten playing in the sand, the lime green ball kicked around as chairs mark goals. I used to play soccer back in elementary unlike Flynn who plaid for our school's varsity team. "Please?"

"Sure," I respond, Flynn taking my hand as he pulls me with him and I forget Augustus, enjoying Flynn as we laugh and smile the whole day.

By sundown the beach is only filled with us recently graduated students, a bonfire beginning as music starts up. I'm next to Flynn in the water, sitting on the opposite end of his board as he sits across from me. Gentle waves push us closer to shore every minute, but the tide pulls us back. Mother loves the tide, how it is a symbol of Selene's love for us werewolves, her creation and children. "Amory?"

Looking back to meet his hunter green eyes, I'm pulled into a gentle and passionate kiss, Flynn pulling me closer as my heart flutters in my chest. I set my hands in his wet hair, pulling gently as he bites my lip gently, moving down to my jaw as I look up to the stars in the sky. He works his way down to my neck, a small moan escaping my lips as I set my hands on his shoulders to pull myself closer to his body. His teeth gently prick my neck, my eyes rolling back as I forget what it symbolizes. As I forget what a small bite to the neck symbolizes. His lips work magic as my wolf loses her mind, howling within me as feelings run south. I pull him closer, pushing my chest upon his own as I lose control.

He pulls back, a smug look upon his face. "You-

I pull him back in for a brief and passionate kiss, one second there and the next gone as his eyes turn dark green. Dark green not in anger, but resembling something more mature.

"You, Amory, are more beautiful than the moon." A blush creeps up upon my cheeks, my head cocking to the side as my eyes widen.

He had playfully bitten my neck. It means something more in werewolf culture than human. It symbolizes someone's want to mate. It symbolizes someone's want to not only mate, but also claim. He wants to claim me as his.

He's moving too fast. Faster than you should as a non-mate. Do I mind? A little because it scares me. It scares me how fast we are moving.

"Are you okay?" He asks, concern lacing his words as I nod my head.

"I'm good, just zones out," I explain, offering Flynn a soft smile as he nods.

"Let's head back to shore."

Within five minutes we are back, the music loud as the group has a bonfire going. We walk up to the group, mingling with everyone as I greet people I haven't seen for what feels like ages.

Green eyes. Bright green and red hair.

"Amory," Molly greets, fixing a smile onto her face as I respect her. She's being mature and not holding a grudge when I would. Hell, if I were her, I would of slapped me by now and taken me down for a fight. "How are you?"

"I'm good. You?" I ask, uncomfortable as Flynn can sense it. I hope Augustus is not here.

"Doing fine." She's broken. She loves Augustus still. Hell. Hell he still loves her. "I see you came here with Flynn." I nod. She's curious as to what went down. I know she is.

"How about you? Who did you arrive with?" I ask, trying to make conversation.

"A-

"You son of a bitch!"

It all happens so fast, how one second Flynn is beside me and the next he's on the ground, Augustus on top of him as he lands a hard punch right to Flynn's jaw. I gasp, watching as Flynn let's Augustus but him again, his head colliding hard with the sand. He's letting him take out some hate before he ends the fight. And he does, easily shoving Augustus off. "This is who you fell in love with, Amory? This dick?! You cheated on me with him!?"

Molly yells at Augustus to calm down.

"Leave it alone, Augustus," I plead, not wanting to see him get hurt.

"You heard her," Flynn snaps, grabbing Augustus's shirt as he stands tall over him. "Leave it alone."

He doesn't. He tries to punch Flynn in the ribs, only for his actions to be stopped and his body thrown onto the sand. "You sure as hell don't want to fight me, Augustus."

"Augustus," Molly calls out. "Let's go."

I interfere, placing my hands upon Flynn as I distance the two of them. "Leave it alone," I whisper, Flynn nodding as he takes my hand, watching as Molly drags Augustus away with her. "We should go too."

"Agreed."

As we are all set in our car and Flynn sits at the wheel, his jaw bruising, his eyes locked upon the parking lot. He seems distant, as if arguing with his wolf. He's distracted and mad. He does not like Augustus at all. We've been sitting here for five minutes now. I make the move, placing my hand upon his cheek as I turn his head to face me. "Flynn, thank you. Thank you for not-

"I wanted to beat him to a pulp, Amory. It took so much to not beat the living shit out of his human ass." I nod, getting closer to Flynn as his breath fans my cheek. "I wanted to."

"Thank you for not," I whisper, placing a light kiss to his purple jaw. "I owe you." He chuckles, nodding in the process.

"I've got an idea." I raise an eyebrow. "One more kiss."

I do, pulling him in for one as he turns off the car, passion filling the kiss as the moonlight streams into the car. Superglue. He's my strength and my weakness...as am I to him. As am I his strength and his weakness.

Chapter 23

I pull him inside, my fingers laced in his shirt as I tug him by it, a soft giggle escaping my lips as he smiles. Flynn takes ahold of my free hand, holding it close as he places a soft kiss upon my lips. With only my car left in the driveway and a note upon the front door, I didn't think. I acted. I acted and here we are two minutes later, the front door shut behind us as I'm pushed gently against the wall right by the stairs. A smile spreads across my face as Flynn places his lips upon my neck, his hands now upon the hem of my shirt, pulling it over my head as my wolf cannot contain her excitement.

As my shirt is on the floor, my hands work fast, taking his off as well. "Tit for tat," I joke, pulling him back against me as Flynn chuckles, the corners of his lips pulling as I can feel them against the flesh of my collarbone. My head rolls back, Flynn pulling away shortly as he hoists my legs around his waist.

He smirks. "Tit-

"Nope," I whisper, knowing he's about to say a dirty joke. He chuckles, going back as he places a kiss upon my lips as I run my hands through his silly locks.

So what note did my parents leave behind? Gone until tomorrow night.

As we make our way upstairs, my bikini top is gone, exposed as I don't feel ashamed like the first few times I had sex. I don't try and cover up anymore or shy away anymore. Why? It's not because I've become accustomed to it. No. It's because of Flynn. It's because Flynn is not about to sleep with me purely for the satisfaction like what we have done with others in the past. Not only is it him, but me too, that we are about to do this because we love one another.

As the bed meets my back and Flynn places himself between my thighs, I know that I will not regret this night. I will not feel ashamed. That I, Amory, know that it's no longer Augustus that I want with me in this form of intimacy, but Flynn.

Flynn. Oh how I'll soon be moaning his name.

The sun is bright, waking me up as my eyes slowly peel open. My arms ache as they stretch, a yawn escaping my mouth as I roll onto my back, the cold hair hitting my bare chest as goosebumps cover my skin. As I reach for the sheets, I find them barely there, all hogged as I turn my head to see Flynn sleeping. He's hogged the blanket and sheets as I lay cold. Taking ahold of the sheets, I gently tug, pulling them over, only for Flynn to roll onto me, those hunter green eyes meeting my own.

"Cold?" He asks, placing a soft kiss upon my temple as he gets up.

Within twenty minutes we're dressed, Flynn borrowing a pair of baggy sweats that reach his mid-shin, an oversized college shirt, and helping me throw the sheets and blanket into the washing machine. Before we shut our eyes last nigh, Flynn dropped the bomb on me, the bomb on me that he will be going to the same university I will be attending as well. Not only did it put a smile on my face, but it caused us to delay shutting our eyes for another hour.

"Was last night all right?" Flynn asks, breaking the silence. I turn my head, looking into his eyes as I nod. "Was it okay? Was I okay? Were you comfortable?"

After all the girls I've seen at school talk about him. Talk about how they would love to know what he's like in bed. What he's like after the deed is done. After all I've heard, I would not expect Flynn to act insecure.

"Amory?" He asks, concern written all over his face as a small smile spreads across my face.

"You were fine-you were better than fine." He nods. Wrapping my arms around his torso, I tilt my head to the side. "You were amazing."

He nods, smiling as he places his hands upon my hips, resting his forehead against my own. "As were you," he responds. "I have to go home today." I'm worried now. Worried about what his father may do. I am frightened of his father. "I am talking with my mother about visiting the college campus." It's a three hour flight to our university.

"Does she want to?" I ask.

"She's interested and open to my idea," Flynn replies. "Could I ask you something?" I nod. "If she's on board, would you want to come along?"

"To Massachusetts? I'd love to." Flynn smiles, the beeping of the washing machine tearing us apart as its time to dry the sheets and blanket. "Will your father be home?" I hate bringing up the topic. We both tense up.

"He should be out on a run today."

"And what if he's home?"

Flynn takes in a deep breath. "I'm going to stand my ground." My skin pales. I'm scared. "I love you, Amory."

I nod. "I love you too."

"I have to face him, you know," Flynn adds. "One day I'll have to stand up to him and-

"And let him know he is not the captain of your fate." Flynn nods. "Of your choices." He takes my hands, backing away as he takes in a deep breath. Flynn let's go of my hands, walking out of the room as he goes to collect the evidence of last night from my parents, my shirt from the floor as well as his. I watch as Flynn places his car keys upon the kitchen counter as I walk out, hoisting himself up to sit upon the granite counter as he looks out the window. I know he wants to stand up to his father, but standing up our culture does not mean talking back and standing firm, but a physical fight. His father would never kill him. His father is the Alpha. Flynn fears that this fight could result in physical pain as well as being made rogue.

Flynn is scared.

Shutting the laundry room door, I walk into the kitchen, tilting my head to the side as he seems distant. I walk up, walking between his legs that dangle from the counter, my hands placed upon his cheeks as I turn his face to mine. "You know that the second I decide to take my own path I will be stripped of the Alpha

title?" I nod. "Tradition is everything to this town and the second I reject tradition people will not respect me anymore."

Respect is everything to an Alpha. Respect is what keeps them satisfied as it's in the blood.

"Do you want to be Alpha?" I ask, knowing the type of question I ask is extremely personal. Flynn meets my gaze, those hunter green eyes filled with sadness. My wolf howls within me, understanding his pain as I just want to see him smile. I just want his eyes to be filled with happiness. I want a smile to grace that face rather than a frown.

Flynn shakes his head. "I don't want to be the next Alpha, but it's my duty, my 'destiny.'" I nod. "But destiny is a silly word for people who are too weak to make their own decisions in life."

Reaching up onto my tiptoes, a I place a soft kiss upon the corner of his lips, feeling him relax under my touch as I can see something once more. I can see that Flynn is who I have fallen for. I can see that Flynn is someone who makes me smile in the morning, who I want to see first thing in the morning, who I want to never watch another frown upon his face.

"When are you heading out?" I ask, my voice soft as I want to not seem him tense up again.

"I have to leave soon," he replies, looking up to the ceiling as I nod.

Hopping off the counter, he pulls me in for a tight hug, bringing me against his chest. "I love you," I whisper, Flynn nodding.

"That's all the hope I need to talk with him."

As I watch Flynn leave, I feel empty as I see his car speed off. Taking a seat upon the couch, I hear the dryer go off, letting me know the load is done as I turn on the TV. I'm scared for Flynn. I'm scared that he could come back bruised and blood, a rogue even. As the dryer beeps again, I let out a shaky breath, heading for the laundry room as Augustus flashes through my mind.

I have to reject him. I should of rejected him before I slept with Flynn last night. Why? Because I had forgotten that when you have sex with anyone not your mate, you feel pain. I out Augustus through pain last night and he has no idea how it happened. I have to reject him. It's not fair. It's not justified. I have to hold myself to the account that I will not be with Flynn again that intimate until I reject Augustus.

As I grab the sheets from the washer, my eyes widen. I gasp, dropping the blankets as I fall to the floor, a sharp pain in my stomach as I cry out in pain. My eyes squeeze shut, my muscles cramping as I roll onto my side. What a coincidence. What irony.

I have to reject him. I have to not only for him, but for me. For this pain. This pain to go away.

I grab my phone, knowing he won't see my text for a while. Unlocking it, my fingers ache as I type away, sending the text to Augustus that should of been sent long age.

We need to talk. ASAP.

Augustus is about to have his reality changed and it's not going to be pretty.

Chapter 24

I stand alone tonight. I stand alone as the woods around me are dark, what looks like could appear in a horror film where monsters lurk. My eyes scan the deserted road before me, my car not here as I ran here in my wolf. My wolf that he will soon greet. I had left my phone at home, realizing it all too late as he should be here any moment now. I'm worried that Flynn is trying to contact me as I wait out here. I'm worried he needs me and cannot reach me.

I can hear a car in the distance, the lights beginning to illuminate the road. My head snaps to the left, watching as his car pulls up next to where I stand. He's going to have questions and I may not be prepared to unleash the answers, but courage is what it takes. If Flynn can stand up to his father today, I can stand up to Augustus today. As his car is shut off and his blue eyes meet mine, a bittersweet feeling settling within my gut. He is about to have his world flipped upside down.

"Amory?" I have a feeling he may even faint. No one has told me how to prepare for this. Not only rejecting someone, but submerging a human barely into the world that I call my own. How am I to handle him? "What's wrong?"

I'm speechless, my throat sour as I have no idea what to say. How do I ease him into this conversation? To this topic? I clear my throat. "How much time do you have?" He raises an eyebrow. I'm already off to a weird start. "Did you experience pain last night? Burning and cramping, your muscles sore, feeling as if your gut is being punched?"

Silence.

He experienced it. He did, I can see it written all over his face. We were once best friends. We know much about one another, especially how to communicate with just one glance. "How the hell would you know that?" He asks, crossing his arms as his tone is negative. He doesn't like this subject.

"Because I felt it today at noon...." He's uncomfortable and I'm just at the tip of the iceberg. "Because I had sex last night you were in pain. Because you has sex today, I was in pain as well."

"What the fuck are you saying? How the hell could you know that I was having sex?" He grabs his keys. I step in front of him, shaking my head. He tries to step around, I stand my ground, grabbing the keys from him. "Amor-

"I'm about to do something and say something that will either cause you to faint, bombard me with questions, run, or never speak to me again."

"Are you stalking me?"

"I'm not close to a stalker," I reply, taking in a deep breath as I get ready for the words I'm about to say. "We are mates. The whole reason why those sparks were present when we kissed was-is all because we are mates." He raises an eyebrow, looking at me as if I am crazy. "I am not human."

"Is Flynn into drugs? Does he smoke a lot? Does he drunk a lot? Are you-

"I'm not human and I'm sober," I state. "I am a werewolf."

He laughs. I know what I'm about to do is a horrible idea.

Taking a step back, I take off my shirt, my sports bra the only thing keeping me distant as Augustus looks at me like I am crazy. I am. I am crazy. Crazy that I am rejecting not only Auguatus today, but tradition over thousands of years old. I look to Augustus as my canines begin to grow, fur sprouting from my limbs, and my bones snapping as they take a different form. I watch as Augustus's eyes widen, watching in complete horror as I shift before his human eyes. Within seconds I am before him in the form of a brown wolf, my paws on the dirt under my claws, Augustus screaming, fainting in seconds as I know this will be a tough day.

Shifting back to human form, I take action, putting on the clothes I saved, I rush over to Augustus. I make sure he's not injured, my heart aching as I know what I am about to do tonight. I rest him against a tree trunk, taking a seat opposite from him as I think of Flynn. I worry about how he's doing. For the next five minutes I wonder how Augustus will wake up, how he will react and see his once best friend turned short-lived girlfriend turned mate and about to be ex-mate.

He wakes up, jerking awake as his eyes widen and his skin pales the second he sees me. Here we go. "You're a werewolf!" I nod. "You're a freaking werewolf and I'm your what, mate? What the hell is that?"

I take in a shaky breath. "We have a connection. Fate paired is hoping we could be the perfect match. Those sparks when we kiss, that's a part of the mate bond," I explain the best that I can. He shakes his head. "The kiss was the thing that started it all for us. The kiss at that one party was what made you leave Molly because of the mate bond. You love Molly."

"No-

"I am a werewolf. Mates are part of culture. Think of it like shipping two people together. It may never said because the sails are damaged. The sails are not even there with us. We were best friends and I wish it could of stayed that way because I see that Molly is who you are meant to be with, not me. Not me." I cry, a sob escaping my lips. "But in all of this I have come to realize that I love Flynn. You, Augustus Brown, love Molly Moore."

He shakes his head. "You're not human."

"No," I whisper. "No. Neither is Flynn."

He nods. He takes in a deep breath. "What do we do? I love Molly and you Flynn. What do we do?"

Here's where the pain kicks in. "It will hurt you physically beyond what you experienced last night..." I pause. "We reject one another." He nods.

"Who does the honors?" I raise my hand, motioning for myself as he accepts it. "Are you sure?"

"Do you love Molly?" He nods. "Do you see a whole future with her?" I ask.

A smile crosses his lips. "I see my world with her."

That's enough evidence. "Then we reject each other," I explain. "Are you ready?"

He gets to his feet and I do as well. "Let's do it..." He trails off, uncomfortable around me as he knows he is not speaking to someone of the same species.

"I, Amory Mifflin, reject Augustus Brown as my mate."

I feel my heart rip in two, pain spreading over my body as I see Augustus' hands become fists as his jaw clenches. I feel as if half of my soul is being lost, disappearing into thin air.

"I, Augustus Brown, rejected Amory Mifflin as my mate."

My room is dark. My room is silent. My room is filled with only myself as I hide under the covers of my bed, my tears dampening the pillow I lay upon. I've been home for thirty minutes now, not even bothering to check my phone as I briefly said hello to my parents. For now I am alone, the pain miserable as my wolf has dug herself a hold and hidden herself in. I want Flynn here. I want him with me, his arms around me, calming me and distracting me from the pain.

I had watched Augustus break down before me, pulling me in for one hug as no longer were the sparks present. We left on terms that his life was changed forever and we were free to make our own destinies. I had watched as he drove off, telling me it would be a while before we would ever talk again. Sadly, I don't blame him, I told him about a world that he thought was just fantasy.

There's a knock at my door, my mother's voice calling me. "Yes?" I ask, holding back my sob as she enters the room, a soft smile upon her face.

"What's this?"

Turning around, my eyes widen to see a black triangle upon a keychain. "Oh, Flynn, I guess it fell off of his keys," I explain, seeing the symbol from House Stark from Game of Thrones. "It must of broken off."

She raises an eyebrow. "Was he here today?"

"Yah," I reply, pushing myself up onto my elbows. "This morning."

"I am also going to guess he was here last night."

"What?" I ask, my eyes widening. "Where would you get the idea that we sleep together?"

Oh Goddess, she will never let this slide if she finds out. "Your sheets and blanket are freshly washed." My skin pales. "Don't worry, I'm glad you're moving on-

"I rejected Augustus today," I interrupt, spilling the information as I watch her face go from smile to a gasp. "We rejected one another," I sob, shooting my hands up to muffle the sound.

"Amory," she gasps, moving fast over to me as she pulls me in for a motherly hug. "Sweetie. I am so-

"I love Flynn," I cry, a smile pulling at my lips. "I freaking love Flynn and I rejected Augustus because he loves Molly and I love Flynn."

She pulls back, shock covering her face as I can see something. I can see she's not surprised though. She looks happy. She looks proud. "You're father owes me twenty bucks. We bet. We bet on when you would come to terms." I smile, laughing softly and in a bittersweet way as she rubs my shoulder. "We knew that you two had something going. Sweetie, I am so sorry about today, but I know that any decision you would make would be one to respect and be proud of."

I nod, wiping away my tears as my phone goes off. Mother moves to check it, her eyes brightening up. "Flynn is calling."

Nodding, I take the phone, watching as she leaves my room, leaving Flynn's keychain in my hand. "Flynn?" I ask, my voice soft as I can hear the soft classic music on the other end. "Are you okay?" I'm concerned now.

He's silent and my heart plummets to my feet.

"Amory."

A car honks outside my window. Turning around, I see his car down below. I get the hint, getting off of my bed, grabbing my jacket, and heading out as I let my mother know. Leaving the house, I head for the car, entering in as Flynn doesn't say a word. He looks ahead, his eyes locked upon the road as his body is tense. "Flynn, are you okay?" I ask, facing him as I am scared. Scared something horrific has happened.

That's when I notice. I notice the bloody knuckles, the dried blood upon his nose, a cut across his eyebrows, and his jaw clenched. My throat runs dry.

"I-I don't know where to start," he whispers, turning to face me as he takes his hand off the wheel and leaves the car in park. "I-I walked into my house and fought with him," he pauses, "mother yelled at him and he threw the first punch. I threw the last punch."

"How did it end?" I ask, my voice laced with concern.

Flynn rests his head back upon the seat. "He is letting me head off to Massachusetts for college. I will work as a computer programmer until he wants to pass down the title."

Flynn got what he wanted. He stood up and convinced his father. I am proud. I am happy.

"Flynn," I whisper, my fingers under his chin as I turn his head to face mine. Our eyes connect and I smile. "I have to tell you something." My eyes begin to water and worry fills his eyes. He shifts his position to fully gave me, his eyes searching my face as a loan tear falls down my face. "I-I rejected Augustus today."

"What?"

"I rejected Augustus," I announce again, Flynn nodding as I notice how close he is. "He rejected me in return." We know what this means. Lips meet mine and my fingers run through his hair, pulling him flush against me as much as I can in this luxury car, needing his arms around me. And his arms envelop me, pulling me closer as I find myself fisting his shirt, needing him. Wanting him. Loving him. "I want you, Flynn. Screw wanting or needing you, I love you. My heart beats faster every time I see you and my wolf does backflips. I want you, all of you, I love you," I announce, getting even more emotional as I wait for Flynn to say something.

"Amory, you have no idea what happens when you walk into the room. I hate leaving this car after it smells like you. I hate leaving you and watching you go home." Flynn shakes his head. "I told my father that I love you tonight. I told him I want to have my future with you and he told me to fuck off. He threw the first punch because I told him I love you." He tucks a loose stand of hair behind my ear. "I see more than months with you. I see more than years with you."

I wrap my arms around his neck. I pull him in for a tight hug. "I see my life with you, Amory Mifflin, and I don't give a damn if my father disapproves." I smile, happier than ever as I pull back, kissing Flynn with such passion that I forget that we are parked right outside my house.

"What do you say?" Flynn asks, pulling back slightly as our eyes lock.

"I don't see days or weeks with you, I don't just see years with you, Flynn, I see the rest of my life with you." He smiles. "I see the rest of my days with you."

CHAPTER 25

"Are you sure everything is in your bag?" Mom asks on the other line, concern in her tone as I roll my eyes.

"I'm pretty sure everything is packed," I reply for her satisfaction, taking ahold of my small luggage as we enter the elevator. My mom wishes me a good next two days, explains for me to enjoy myself and not do anything dumb, to call her every night, and not run off and get drunk. "Love you too," I close the call with her, placing my phone back in my jacket as an arm wraps around my shoulder. "So we visit tomorrow?" I ask, refreshing my tired mind on the plan as Flynn nods.

Luna Willow is with us, dressed in a beautiful pale pink dress, her hair pinned back in a bun, and flawless. Part of the Luna's duty is to be the face of the pack, to dress appropriately and show other packs how they pack holds them self. How Luna Willow dressed let's other packs know we are powerful and friendly, open to new partnerships, but we are not to be disappointed. If people say Alpha Cade, they would see a pack of warlords for generations to come. If they truly saw the Alpha family, they would see a mess struggling to keep their mask from falling off. "Amory, are you excited?" Luna Willow asks, offering me a soft smile as I nod.

"Very, I've wanted to visit for a while now. Since I know I am going here it makes it even better," I reply, looking to Flynn as a small smile tugs at his lips. "Just sad how far it is from home." Although it's a negative aspect for me, I know Flynn is more that pleased to be states away from our home state. He's happy to be far away from his father.

As the elevator dings, we exit, walking down the long and glamorous hall to our room. Luna Willow refused to take money for the hotel or even the ticket up here, saying to take it like a graduation present from here. A very massive graduation present as we flew first class and I am now in one of the most expensive hotels in the location. The room has two King-sized beds and a couch. Naturally Luna Willow told Flynn that he would be taking the couch, as both her and I will be taking the beds. She knows we are dating and respects that, but Flynn and I also know to respect her. My respect for her skyrocketed as I saw her true loyalty for the pack, how she still keeps it together when we husband has another woman. She keeps it together when her husband is furious. But my respect for her is not the highest, as I have never seen her stand up to her husband about the issues. Yes, I've watched her force her husband into apologizing before the whole pack to his son, but if she is so strong, why can't she stand up for herself? Because she knows doing that could result in divorce or the pack splitting in two. Sometimes I see her as weak, but then I notice that she puts up with what she does because she loves her pack.

As Luna Willow unlocks the door, I turn to Flynn, seeing him texting someone very quickly. Looking away, I focus my attention upon my home for the next two nights, knowing that mother will want me to thank Luna Willow every day and night for this opportunity.

By the end of the night, I've brushed my teeth, washed my hair, and have changed into shorts and an old shirt, the Luna strolling out of the bathroom and to her bed as I can hear the city just outside. The lights of the city disappear as she shut the curtains, wishing me a good night as she climbs into her bed. Within five minutes she's fast asleep as I sit at the desk, the screen of my phone the only light as I know just behind the door to my left is where Flynn is. He's awake, I am fully aware as I can hear his music playing. We made a plan this evening at dinner. Thankfully it just happened to be a great plan because the Luna takes medical drugs prescribed to her to fall asleep fast and stay asleep. Flynn was basically on cloud nine the second he remembered that factor.

I softly open the door, moving past it fast as I shut it softly. The second the door is shut, I turn around to have my clothes thrown at me. Grabbing ahold of the clothing articles, I look up to see Flynn, smiling as he's all set for the night, nothing that you would expect someone like him to wear for a walk downtown, but presentable. Sweatpants and a soccer shirt from his select team, his hair messily combed back, and his green eyes bright with excitement.

I'm quick to change, a pair of dark wash jeans now on my legs, a somewhat sheer, navy blouse covering my top as the shirt has a V in the back and somewhat low front. "Ready?" Flynn asks, followed by a nod from me as I pull my hair back into a bun. He takes my hand, pulling me with him as I cover my mouth to muffle a giggle. Sneaking out and exploring the city about a five minute walk from campus.

As we exit the hotel, my eyes light up, the signs once just plain colors are now neon and flashy, people once dressed in business attire are now replaced with individuals either dressed for a casual walk or a fun night on the town. Street performers can be found on every street, flashy cars driving by, and the night life alive as Flynn guides me across the street. "It's beautiful," I comment, pulling him closer to my side as he takes us somewhere I don't know where. "What's the place you had in mind?"

"You'll see," he replies. Flynn picks up his pace, causing us to jog a tad across a block. As we talk a sharp left turn, he picks me up, swinging me around twice as a laugh escapes my lips. Setting me back down onto my feet, he takes my hand again, pulling me with him as I cannot help but let my smile grow even wider. "We are almost there."

I'm speechless.

"Goddess, it's beautiful," I whisper in awe, looking out upon the view before me. As we stand on the ledge of the balcony of the hill the city has been built upon, I gaze in awe of the stars above and the city lights below. The architecture is amazing, modern yet elegant, streets winding up the hill, the lights bright, soft jazz filling the air, and a river just beneath us. It looks like it came out of a paining you would find in the Great Gatsby, what West Egg would look like in modern times and crammed in the city. It's beautiful. Bridges cross the river to the other side, bridges for cars and for people as well, a few boats you would find in Venice, Italy are located in the water as well, a few couples enjoying a night out.

"Flynn..." I trail off, looking up to him as I find he's been looking at me, a soft gaze held with mine as my heart races and my wolf does a backflip. "Thank you." He smiles, lowering his head to mine as his lips capture my own in a beautiful kiss. His hands are upon my waist, pulling me closer as his touch is gentle. My hands find his neck, lightly placed upon the back as I pull him closer as well.

As the soft jazz fills the air, he spins me around, a smile tracing my lips as I know I was right to say the those words. Those words that I don't just see days, weeks, or months with this man, but my life. In my own way, I was Augustus. Augustus was in love with Molly when his mate was beside him all along. Sure, we rejected one another, but the similarities still are present. I was in love with Augustus when Flynn was by my side all along, it just took me the right prescription of glasses to see that.

Pulling away, Flynn laces his fingers with mine, his arms wrapped around me as we stay in one another's embrace. I rest my head against his shoulder, looking out to the view I would love to see as a painting. Just looking at the view seems as if you're escaping reality. It's a dream. It's beautiful.

"What do you say about a late night snack?" He asks.

Within fifty minutes we are back in the hotel, walking through the marble lobby as we head for the elevator. Hardly anyone is out in the hotel, a few late swimmers chatting and a couple of staff polishing the tables for tomorrow. As we enter the elevator and no one else comes in, the second the doors close, I look to Flynn. "Thank you for tonight. It was amazing."

He smirks as I've helped to inflate his ego that's already big enough. "I knew you'd love it," he comments, watching as I take a step closer to him.

"We're on the twelfth floor, correct?" I ask.

He nods, raising an eyebrow.

I grab him by the collapse of his shirt, pulling him to me as my lips lock with his. My hands are on his check, feeling him as his hands are on either side of me on the walls of the elevator. For what seems like years we stay in one another's embrace, lips locked as our wolves battle for dominance. My back is cold as its pressed up against the metal walls, goosebumps forming over my skin as I wrap my arms around his neck, trying to eliminate any space between the two of us.

The second the elevator comes to a stop, we pull apart, lungs dying for air as we take in deep breaths.

As we head back to our room, we whisper, knowing to be quiet just in case. The second the room door opens and we are in, the darkness swallows us, Flynn tripping over what I could only guess is a table. A giggle escapes my lips as he plummets to the floor, crashing as a loud thump fills the air. I crack up, my hands flying up to cover my laughs as there's no sound from Luna Willow's part of the hotel room. Flynn groans, but he doesn't get up, rather grabbing my arm as he pulls me down to the floor, right onto him as my eyes widen. "You're gonna wake up your mother," I comment, straddling the future Alpha as he smiles. "Besides, we have a big day tomorrow."

"You win," he whispers, helping me up to my feet as we both know we have to be well rested for tomorrow. "See you in the morning." Nodding, I wave bye, sliding past the door and into the other side of the room, changing quickly back into my sleeping attire. The second I'm in bed and tucked away for the night, I hear the Luna move in her bed.

"You love him, don't you?" She asks, her voice scratchy as she's just woken up. "Amory?"

A smile pulls at my lips as my heart warms up. "I do. I love him."

She lets out a sigh, still half asleep. "No one has ever told him that beside me." My throat runs dry. "No one has ever truly loved him but me." Silence as my heart breaks for Flynn. "I can tell he loves you too."

CHAPTER 26

Beautiful. The buildings are a traditional style, the bricks more than a century old, the windows long and narrow, and massive trees that shade the sidewalks. The entire university is beautiful to look at, the whole day spent touring as the weather is beautiful. If anything, I cannot wait for the next chapter of my life to begin here.

The next chapter as I set forth on my passions and dreams as Flynn is beside me, going to the same university. Only, there's a difference between us, how one is free to study what they want and have the respect of their parents. How one is tied down, knowing that their dreams will be short lived as soon they will have to face the reality that a parent wants them to face.

"Really excited for all of this," I mention, turning to Flynn as we stand at the top of the stairs to the university's most famous building that overlooks the fresh green grass and students still here for summer that pass by. "Two months away."

"Two months," Flynn agrees, a smile upon his face as his mother is at the end of the stairs, capturing pictures of the school as she's been sending them to her sisters all day, bragging about her son. "Amory?" Flynn paused, looking back to the building behind us as the sun begins to set. "What if I told you that I don't want to be Alpha. That I don't want to take my father's place and run the pack." To werewolves, this decision is more important than the decision to get married.

"I would respect you because it requires so much time and patience to make that choice. I know that if that is what you truly want, then don't let it weigh you down," I reply, taking ahold of his hands. "Do you want to be Alpha?"

Flynn smiles, trying to combat the emotions with the pearly white flash of teeth as my heart swells. "I've never wanted it."

"Then don't sell yourself a unhappy future. Act upon your beliefs."

Flynn looks to his mother below, his eyebrows furrowing together as he watches her snap another picture. "She loves my father still after everything that has happened. She loves him and I can not fathom how she does," he whispers, pulling me in for a tight hug as I can tell he is suffering. "I fear that moving away for college...I cannot protect her from him." He pauses. "But I've never had to protect her before. She's always stood up herself."

She's never left him.

"My mother puts our pack right after me. She would rather face my father's wrath than leave our pack." I nod, watching as Luna Willow waves to us, a smile plastered across her face. "She really likes you, you know," Flynn comments. "She thinks of you as a daughter more than anything." My heart clenches.

"Does she know you don't want to be the next Alpha?" I ask, taking Flynn's hand as we walk down the steps.

"I think that deep down she knows, she just doesn't want to come to terms with it." I understand where Luna Willow could be coming from, how she would rather ignore the truth until the time comes for her reality to be shaken. We walk down, greeting the Luna as she talks about the plans for the rest of the day. We have a twenty minute walk back to our rental car and a short drive after that back to the hotel. Tonight Luna Willie plans on us dining out and then getting some sleep as we have an early flight tomorrow. "Did you like it?" Flynn asks his mother, watching as her face lights up as she rants about how beautiful the campus is and how well of a fit it is as well. If anything, I wonder what life will be like without her son. She's already lost one of her children, and the second Flynn tells her he does not want to be Alpha, how will she feel?

Walking through the campus, Flynn is beside me the whole time, the two of us excited for what the next four years hold. As the city gets closer and so does our parking spot, I look back to the college, knowing many memories will soon be made.

Once we are back in the city, we drive to a local restaurant that Luna Willow read about in a magazine, a restaurant located in the heart of the city. From throwing darts to playing pool to even just sitting down with family, it has what I would say sounds like a good time. The second we enter the building, the countless sounds of chatter and plates clinking together fill the air as we are seated immediately thanks to reservations. We take our seats, Flynn leaving to go and take care of a call as I am left alone with Luna Willow.

"He really likes you," she comments, smiling as she starts our conversation. I nod, looking over my shoulder to see Flynn outside, talking on the phone as my heart warms up. Just by looking at him my legs feel like jelly and my wolf does backflips. Turning back around, Luna Willow takes out her wallet, pulling what appears to be a picture from the small wallet. "This was Flynn at four years old, he was a little troublemaker."

I smile, looking at the young Flynn as his black hair is messy and wet as he holds the hose in his tiny hands. His green eyes look just past the camera to who I suppose is Luna Willow, a bright smile upon his face as he looks authentically happy. Before I was with him in a relationship, I had seen him smile, but never to were it seemed authentic. I had seen him smile on rare occasions, after a run or when a joke was told, but they never seemed real, as if he was forcing himself to use those facial muscles to sell a small lie. But now I see him smile more than ever, how every time they brighten my day as I just want that smile to be there forever.

"He's very tiny," I comment, knowing that now he is tall and built very nicely.

"He was very small until high school," the Luna adds. "His wolf was tiny too. I had a fear that he would grow up to be an omega." My skin pales for a mother to admit this to anyone, it's a big deal. It shows upmost respect. "He has Alpha blood yet I thought he could be the runt of the pack. Look at him now for goddess sake, he's tall and will be the next Alpha." I nod, looking back to Flynn as I no longer see him on his phone, but looking across the busy street. He's looking at something, but the cars passing by cover my view.

I raise an eyebrow, wondering what he sees as he sprints across the street, dodging cars as I stand up a bit in my seat. "Are you okay?" Luna Willow asks, concern laced in her words as I turn back around to face her. Is he in trouble? Did something happen? I'm scared.

"I-I need to go and check on Flynn I think...just see how he's doing," I whisper, the Luna nodding her head with suspicion as I take off.

Everything moves slow, how I take ever step closer to the outside as he's across the street now, frozen in place as I see his mouth move. By the time my hands wrap around the metal door handles and I push the restaurant doors open, I meet the crowd of the city. It's hard to see, pushing my way up the traffic of people as I try and see what is going on. Maybe I'm making a big deal out of nothing? Maybe something could be wrong? My eyes become like a tunnel, everything else blurred as only Flynn is clear. My eyes begin to feel pressure, my heart rate speeding up as I can hear the blood rushing in my ears.

I meet the end of the sidewalk now, a good glance on Flynn as he still moves his mouth. Waiting for the walking light to turn white, my nerves skyrocket as I don't know what is happening. The second the light turns white, I walk, my feet numb as I see him move and before my eyes is the most gorgeous woman I've ever seen.

Within raven-black hair that frames her oval face with soft curls, fair skin, a slender yet toned body, golden eyes, and a light dusting of freckles, she belongs on the cover of a magazine. She's everything I am not. She's grace and beauty, she's poise and elegance, and she's got a beautiful look to her. She's what girls strive to be when they are growing up and who people my age are jealous of.

She's who I could never be to him.

I watch as she pulls him in for a hug, tears forming as she holds him close, her arms wrapped around his strong frame as my throat runs dry. Once again, I am the other woman. I'm just the obstacle to their Prince Charming. I'm the ugly witch or dragon that has to be slaughtered like an animal for their dreams to come try.

She moves back from Flynn, saying words as he puts his hands in his pockets. He's nervous. As she offers him a lopsided smile, I watch as she kisses his cheek, looking to his eyes with tears in her own.

It's as if time has escaped them.

My heart breaks as I watch him pull her in for one last hug, saying words to her he may never tell me again as I feel the first tear slide down my cheek.

She is who I could never be to him. She is his mate.

Just as I am about to turn back, I watch as he lets go of her, nodding to a male that is standing by a parked car on the side of the road. The mystery man nods back, the woman leaving Flynn for the make as Flynn waves bye to the two of them. I catch view of the woman, of her hand, the ring upon her finger as I feel hope beginning to form within my chest.

Flynn turns around, waking back the way he came. Just as he looks up, our eyes meet, locked as my skin pales.

Time is nonexistent as he runs to me through the sea of people, reaching out for me as I stand frozen, not knowing what to expect.

He takes me, his hands in either side of my face as he pulls me in for a beautiful kiss, my body electrified as I close my eyes.

"Amory," he whispers, placing a kiss on the corner of my mouth. "Amory, I love you so damn much."

My heart melts.

"What was her name?" I ask, knowing the delicacy of the subject.

He shakes his head, leaning his forehead upon my own. "June, and she wanted to reject before I even told her," he pauses, taking in a deep breath. "She said the moment she saw me heading over to her, she knew I loved someone else and she told me she already found her special someone."

I smile as I know Flynn did this for him, for us, for me. He is in pain just as I was when I rejected Augustus, and just like Flynn, I will be there the whole journey as he feels his soul splitting into two. "I love you," I whisper, kissing his cheek as I pull away softly. "Now, your mom is waiting for us and is getting worried."

Flynn nods, looking at me with what I can only describe as adornment as he takes my hand. "Lets go then," he whispers, taking my hand as I look back to the car, looking at June. June, the woman I will never know but will always want to thank. June, the woman who had every right to my man but knew he loved someone else just as she did.

She waves to me, smiling as I nod back to her, offering her a smile as we both know this is the only time we will ever see one another. All we need is an acknowledgment of one another to be satisfied, knowing that we are happy with how fate has been defied and choices have been made.

As I look back to Flynn, I know one truth: I want to spend the rest of my life with him.

Chapter 27

I don't know what to do exactly. Do I tell him everything is going to be fine or that he did the right thing? Both of these can be taken to extreme ways beyond me trying to comfort him. My eyes take a short glance to Flynn, how he sits beside me, his eyes locked upon the road, the radio off, and it seems as if he's absent. He's feeling the side effects of rejecting your mate, how you feel emptiness, lost as you become vulnerable and your heart aches. Flynn got me through much of how I felt, how I was heartbroken and he was beside me, knowing to not take advantage of my vulnerability as he respected my state of being.

His jaw is clenched, his hands wrapped tight around the wheel as the familiar landscapes surround me. Just an hour ago we arrived back in the airport we left from, a hour drive before us the minute we landed. Luna Willow has business in the city, already having driven separate to the airport, meaning that it's just Flynn and I. It's been thirteen hours since Flynn was rejected and he rejected June. June, the woman Flynn was destined to be with and he will never truly know. My mate I know, my mate I was best friends and I ruined that also shattered his reality. I want to check up on Augustus, to make sure he's okay, but I know to give him time. Time before I pull him aside and introduce him to this new reality of werewolves. Why? Because I have to show him we pose as no threat to him, we are peaceful and just trying to get through life as he is as well. It will take time, but I also want to make sure that he does not go spilling the information to everyone. Hunters are here in our world, though they only hunt down werewolves who threaten the minds of humans, the mind that think the supernatural are fairytales.

Looking back to Flynn, I want to say something. Something related to yesterday's events, but at the same time I want to respect his personal space. His little bubble that he keeps himself within right now, living in a different kind of reality as he blocks out the world around him and keeps focused on his emotions. Do I blame him? I don't. Resting my head against the window, I look out at the familiar views as we get closer to the inevitable. I don't know what exactly to say.

"Pull over." I don't know what I just said, only aware that I had no filter and do not know where that came from.

His eyes meet mine and I know that I said the wrong thing right away. A cold stare is all I get, his jaw clenched as his knuckles turn white as they grip the wheel tighter. He's broken. "Pull the car over," I repeat, keeping my voice strong as on the inside I'm shaking and scared. Scared not because he would hurt me, but scared because I do not know what I am about to do.

Flynn complies, pulling car off the freeway and to the country road. I have no idea where we are, but I know if I decide to run home in wolf form, I'll find a way back home. As Flynn puts the car in park and the atmosphere becomes more tense than ever, I take in a deep breath.

Looking to Flynn, I run a hand through my hair in stress. "When Augustus started to fall in love with Molly, my wolf dug herself a hole within my mind. As they continued their relationship, my wolf refused to come to me, to talk with me, or to even shift," I explain, not knowing why I am telling Flynn this. "People started asking questions, even you, as to why I was not going on the typical day runs, and that made me feel pointless. Without my wolf or mate I felt like I had no true purpose." I lean my head back, my breath shaky. "The day you punched that junior and told me off, I was so angry. I was frustrated and heartbroken." Flynn's eyes soften. "That day I shifted because your comments were the last straw for me, my wolf knowing that a shift and long run was what we needed to get through the day. She knew she could not run forever like how I was running from the truth that my mate did and does love someone else."

Flynn takes in a deep breath. "I'm still sorry about that day, the words that I had said."

"When I rejected Augustus, I asked him if he loved Molly," I add. "I asked him and he said he saw his future with her. I didn't need to hear that for validation that he loves her, but because he needed to hear it. To hear it because I wanted him to know that he doesn't love me but Molly, that the mate bond was the only thing that caused him to think of me romantically." My phone rings buzzing in my pocket as it interrupts the moment of confession.

As my eyes shift down to where my phone is, I jump in surprise as his hand wraps around mine. Looking up to Flynn, I catch his eyes, the stare gone as he holds a soft glance. He pulls my hand to his lap, warmth spreading in my heart as Flynn opens his mouth. "The moment I saw June I knew how it would end," Flynn whispers. "As a kid, I knew my parents were mates, and watching them together made me dislike the idea. My whole life I've wanted to fall in love like humans, not with destiny or fate, but by choice." He turns off the engine. "The second I saw June I knew we would have a relationship like my parents if we chose the path of destiny. I knew that we would become uninterested with each other in due time." My throat becomes dry. "The second I saw her, I didn't find myself zoned in on her and head over heels, but you flashed through my mind."

A warm hand brushes past my cheeks, my heart skipping a beat. "June told me that I could never be happy with her." He pauses. "I was scared she would not understand that I wanted a rejection."

I smile, watching as his lips pull up into a soft smirk at my reaction. "I love you," I whisper, my voice soft as I take ahold of Flynn's hand that rests upon my cheek. Kissing his knuckles, I take ahold of the opportunity of the moment, leaning over as I place a kiss upon his lips. As I pull away, I keep my eyes trained upon Flynn's as he smiles.

With one glance, we decide to head on back to our town, knowing we still have a drive along the way. Flynn turns on the radio, the classic rock filling the car as he taps his hands on the wheel and I tap my foot to the beat. As the trees go by and we soon see the sign to town, I watch as Flynn turns tense. His father is mad at him. Luna Willow will be back home soon. She's never been hit or anything, but I fear that when Flynn leaves, what will happen.

As we pull up in front of my house, I see my parents to be gone, looking forward to hopping into bed and sleep from the trip. "See you tomorrow?" I ask, remembering how Luna Willow wanted me to come over for dinner within a little less than twenty-four hours. Flynn nods, saying goodbye just as I grab the handle of the door. Right as I open the door, my arm is grabbed lightly, pulling me back into my seat as I raise an eyebrow.

"I've made my decision," Flynn whispers, his tone serious as I fear for what he is about to say. "About being the next Alpha."

"What did you decide?" I ask, knowing that this is a massive life choice. Not only will it affect him, but his family, as well as his pack.

He turns off the music and runs a hand over his face, pinching the bridge of his nose.

"I will not become Alpha."

I don't want him to go home. I don't want him to let his father know without his mother or even me there. I don't want him to face his father because I am scared of what could happen.

Flynn closes his eyes, concentrating on calming his nerves down as I am scared. "What are you going to do?" I ask.

"I'm going to let him know soon enough. I know he will cut me off and made me a rogue, but I truly don't give a damn." I nod. "It is best for the pack as well. I am not made to be an Alpha, my sister was to be the true Alpha. My Beta will take the role and I plan on creating my future outside of the wolf world." Few make the decision to do something like this. "What do you think?"

I'm speechless. I'm proud. I'm scared.

"I am happy for you," is all I say, knowing that I am happy for him, that this is what he wants. "I am terrified for you, but I am happy more than ever because this is what you want and I believe in you."

He smiles, pulling me close as I know I am truly happy for him.

"Amory?" I nod, meeting those beautiful hunter green eyes. "I want to ask you something. I don't want an answer at all right away because this takes much thought." He has my every nerve going crazy as my fingers begin to shake. "Promise me?"

I nod. "I promise." He pulls back, his stare intense.

"If I am made a rogue, would you be willing to leave the pack to be with me?" I know what this means. If he is banished by his father, those who associate themselves with him will also be banished. If he is vanished and I still continue a relationship with him, I will be banished. Not only does it mean becoming a rogue, but this means more than that. It means that he basically loves me enough that he's doing an early proposal. It's an early proposal, informal and a massive decision.

Flynn is practically asking if I would be willing to throw away my reality and one day marry him.

"Flynn-

"Take as long as you need for your answer because it's not an easy decision," Flynn interrupts. I nod, knowing this is where we end our conversation as I hop out of the car, watching as he drives off as I am left speechless.

Speechless and unsure.

Flynn wants to marry me. What do I want? I have no idea.

Chapter 28

The weather is beautiful at this time in the morning, the dew fresh from the night, the sun barely rising, the chirping of birds heard, and the town barely awake in this summer day. Here I sit, on the patio of the backyard, my mother beside me as we enjoy early morning coffee with one another. As we discuss how my life is about to do a three-sixty with college alone, I have so much I have to tell her. Last night I had asked if she wanted an early morning cup of coffee with me to discuss some issues. Starting off the conversation about college, we are still on the topic, right now talking about my roommate who I will meet in person when I arrive. Mother is in for big news. News that happened three days ago and I've been reflecting off of. For three days my mind has been busy, my eyes unable to rest at night as I can't calm myself down.

Flynn respects that, giving me time as we text here and there, for the most part a sense of me avoiding him has settled in my stomach. Avoiding not because I have made my decision and it's a definite no, but because it's a massive decision. To put your needs before the packs is all tradition warns you about. The strength of the wolf is the pack and vice versa. As children, we are taught that our own dreams and wishes are selfish, that if we head off to college and never return to the pack, we are banished and seen as tainted and selfish. The second you put what is best for you before your pack is when you watch those with strong beliefs in tradition shun you. Thankfully my parents have always been open, teaching me along the way that I can have a life outside the pack. Rogues are seen as negative for the most part, but only those that are banished. A majority of rogues decide to leave not because of a bad relationships to the pack because they wish to see the world, to experience what the humans have done, to see out their ambitions. Change is something you cannot avoid. Our community likes to ignore the rapid change happening all around and because of that, we still hold onto viewpoints that put us behind in developments of ideas. The strongest packs in our Empire are built off of loose traditional views.

"So I have some news," I interrupt the silence as we finish talking about my roommate. My mother nods her head, taking a sip of her coffee as she's intrigued. Little does she know that what she will hear are big words. Setting my cup down on the table, I pull my knees into my body, trying to ind a comfortable position for this uncomfortable topic. "Flynn...he found his mate."

Her eyes go from bright and interested to emotionless. She doesn't know what to expect from what I will say. Running a hand through my hair, a ghost smile passes my face. "I watched him meet her, June, a beautiful woman. She was breathtaking and everything I thought as a perfect girl for Flynn."

My mother nods. "Amory, sometimes the perfect girl is not the perfect match," she inputs, watching as my eyes water and I wipe away the fresh and salty tears.

"He, well, she rejected him first." My mother's eyes widen. "She's in a relationship and in love with a man. Flynn confided in me that some of the words she spoke were that she knew from the way Flynn looked at her that he was in love with someone else."

"That someone else being you," she comments, watching as I nod as my smile spreads. "Sweetie, are you doubting that h-

"He informally proposed to me the day we got back."

I have no filter, letting my mother know the main reason I wanted to sit down with her and have a chat. I watch as she goes from caring and motherly to shocked and speechless. I watch as her mouth is open, unable to form words as her eyes are wide. When I was young father said I knew how to shock people news, I guess this is a perfect paradigm.

"Flynn wants to reject the Alpha title. He plans on doing if before he leaves for university and we both know his father will banish him because of it." I take in a shaky deep breath. "He wants to know if I would be still willing to stand by his side when he's a rogue." To werewolves, this is an informal proposal as well as very early.

Early as in this summer we just started to be part of a beautiful relationship that I see continuing for years to come.

Mom takes my hand, squeezing it as she offers me a soft smile. "Do you love Flynn?"

"I do, I see so much of my life with him, but it's just that he came out of the blue with the informal proposal," I explain. "I don't know whether I'm scared or just still shocked that I have not gone to him and given him an answer. This is not an easy answer, but I know it will truly shape my future. I have feeling and thoughts about what happens if he grows tired of me or I of him, if we end up hating one another. There are so many things I do not know what could happen because we just began this relationship about a month ago."

At a month most middle school couples have split. At a month most lower-class men in secondary school are posting about their one-month anniversary on social media. A month is just a fraction of a year and barely a slice of a lifetime.

But I love him. I love him and pretty much all middle school couples do not mean those words when they tell them to their partner. I love him and I even rejected my mate because I was in love with him.

"What do you want? Do you want to continue your relationship with him or leave it be? You don't have to decide if you want to marry him, but if you see a future with him, set that as the first guideline." I nod. "You two are going to the same college, so that can help your relationship. Say that you want to continue your relationship and you want to be in the boyfriend and girlfriend stage longer just to get a feel for it all before jumping to being his fiancé." I know what she is saying, how I tell him I want to be with him and am willing to be made rogue with him, but I want this phase of our relationship to last longer. Will he understand? He should. He will. He will respect what I say and also know that what I am saying shows that we have a future with one another.

"Thank you," I whisper, my voice weak as those hunter green eyes flash through my mind. "I love him, I love Flynn and I know that he loves me just as much." Mom smiles, pulling me in for a hug as the sun rises a bit more.

"And I can see that you two do love one another," she adds, causing a smile to spread widely across my face. She knows that those words will only bring me joy because they are the truth. The truth I was so blind that I almost didn't get to experience. "Now, sadly I have work to head off to, but while I'm gone, I want you to know that I think you should let Flynn know the recent news."

I agree one hundred percent.

If anything that I found out interesting as I grew up was how my parents raised me. While many times I would visit friends and have conversations with their parents, I always found a certain pressure upon my friend. The parents constantly pressed their child on the topic of a mate or serving the pack for their future. While many of my friends wee signed up for camps to train with warriors or the pack or nursery care for the pups, I spent my summers at camps where artistic crafts and skits were a main focus as well as fun days experiencing nature the way humans saw it. I remember once when I was sixteen, how I watched one of my friends leave the pack for a special warrior training program across the seas, her parents expressing their dreams of how she will one day be a Royal Guard for the Alpha King. I remember my friend confessing to me the night before how she just wanted to be a teacher, living in a busy city.

She never got her dream.

As for me, my parents always taught me that your dreams are just as important, that your voice will not be silenced by the traditional viewpoints in our culture.

I guess my parents made me stronger, strong enough that I now stand where I do, my nerves skyrocketing as I know what I am about to do could be seen as insane. Taking in a shaky deep breath,

I hear the footsteps draw closer, the pine scent getting stronger as the sunlight streams in through the massive windows that were specifically placed by extraordinary architects. I know what I am about to do...if words gets out, many could look away from me or walk on the other side of the street. Why? I am about to talk with Alpha Cade.

"Ms. Amory, what do I owe this visit?" He asks, taking a seat at his mahogany desk as my throat runs dry. I know that he shut the door, Flynn on the other side of the door as he watched me go in without aid, facing his father. Many would not dare even think of inviting themselves into the Alpha's office unless with urgent news. I guess I am thankful for that.

"I am here to say that I love your son."

He rolls his eyes. "You are pathetic. The only person I will allow to love my son the way you think you do is the woman who will become this packs next Luna!" His words sting. Sting because he says I should not love his son because I am not fit. "My son is the next Alpha of this pack and I'll be damned the day I see someone of your status in this pack even sleep in the same bed as him." Oh the what he doesn't know. "He does not need your fangirl love. You just want the Luna positio-

"The position of Luna means nothing to me and I would not give a damn if Flynn was an omega. I would still say that I love him."

I know Flynn can hear every word spoken in these four walls. But that doesn't shift how I talk, it only makes me talk louder to claim how much I love him and care for him.

"You're just like every whore, claiming you do not care for being Luna." My jaw clenches.

"I rejected my mate for Flynn and I will be damned the day I look back and think that it was a bad idea," I snap, my wolf infuriated as I want to bang his head upon his desk. "No words that you speak from your filthy mouth can affect the feelings I have for Flynn, the male outside who you do not deserve one bit to call your flesh and blood."

Alpha Cade rises to his feet, his wolf wanting to rip me in two. "You're insane to talk to your Alpha with that tone and words," he growls, the walls shaking. "You should be pissing you pants."

I chuckle. "Please, rejecting my mate was harder than this," I add, my wolf feeling empowered as we talk to the Alpha with such a tone. "After everything you have done to Flynn, how you try and dictate his life, beat him, and even try to tell me how to feel, you deserve no respect from me. You cheat on your mate and make your family suffer as this pack is somehow supposed to look up to you, that is all just a smorgasbord of messed up!" I growl, watching as the Alpha tries so hard not to kill me or banish me. But I know and he knows that the second he banishes me, Flynn will leave to be with me.

Flynn would become rogue to spend his dying days with me as I will do for him. As I will do for him.

"You have no place here," Alpha Cade snaps, taking a seat as he motions for me to leave. He doesn't want me anywhere near him every again.

"No, I do not. I do not have anyplace in a room where a deceiver and miserable man runs a pack blind to how bad their leader is."

"Get out!" He booms. "Leave! You have no place to say anything."

I hold my head high. "You're right. But guess what, Alpha," I announce, heading for the door of the office. Smiling, I tilt my head to the side. "When Flynn and I are sending out of wedding invitations, we will make sure that your name is not included whatsoever."

With that, I leave, knowing my answer to Flynn's proposal as well as knowing that the big bad wolf can be out in his place. After all, I did this more than for just me, more than for just Flynn, but for our relationship. Our relationship that I am ready to watch blossom into something magical.

CHAPTER 29

Trouble in paradise. Trouble in a relationship where two saw their futures take shape together. As the rain pours down on this summer evening, I watch as she hops out of the car, pacing herself quickly over as I wonder what went wrong. I wonder what happened to cause her to come here, to the house where the girl that he cheated on her with lives. She should hate me, never want to venture to this property, yet here she is, soaking wet and looking heartbroken. Getting up from my seat, I head to the front door, hearing her knock three times. A short pause and I open the door, meeting those bright green eyes as I do not know what to expect. Do I expect a slap, vulgar words thrown left and right, or what else? She should hate and I know I deserve it, yet something tells me that she came here because she needs my help.

"Amory," Molly greets, her voice shaky as I open the door wide, motioning for her to enter as she stands out in the rain.

"Hi, Molly," I greet, closing the door behind her as I look at her appearance. Her red hair is one massive birds nest, bags under her green eyes, her skin paler than usual, and her posture slouched unlike the poise posture she usually cares herself around with. I remember one of the first things I became jealous of was how she holds her shoulders back and her chin high as if natural, I thought that was a reason why Augustus loved her over me. "Can I help you?" I ask, trying not to sound rude as her eyes begin to water. "Are you-

I'm silenced not by a slap, but by pure shock as she throws her arms around me, latching herself onto me as a sob escapes her lips. Instantly I wrap my arms around her, comforting her as I am worried about what is happening to her. She's heartbroken. Something bad has happened and I have a good idea that it has to deal with Augustus.

"I need help," she whispers, her voice hoarse as I don't know if I will be able to help.

"Ask away." I owe her at least that much.

"Since you two split, he's been different...he's been cautious and has been going into the woods a lot," Molly explains as I hand her the cup of coffee. "We hardly talk or see one another. He's become a hermit and is obsessed with these weird books." I already know what is going on and I feared it would happen. I knew it would happen, but I feared that it would get this bad. I mean, what do you expect when you submerge a human into a whole new world of wolves and the stuff humans claim are nightmares. So fee humans submerged into our world are able to not go as crazy on the reading up. Hell, some humans go insane.

I owe it to Augustus. I owe it to him to help him, to talk with him. "Where is he?" I ask, taking in a deep breath as Molly shakes her head. "I can help and chat with him, Molly."

She wipes away a tear. She loves him. I know she does. "My guess is that he's in his room. He's there when he's not in the woods. I'm worried, Amory, and I am here because I know, that behind all of this drama, you two are still best friends." Her words feel like knives. Knives not because I want to be something more than a best friend like how I wanted in the past, but knives because after everything I've done to her, she still finds kindness and respects me. "Please."

I nod. "I'll help. Don't worry. I'll have a chat with him," I inform, knowing its best to hold it off till Molly decides to leave. I don't want to kick her out when she needs someone, for she has never kicked me out. Months ago I saw Molly as a girl I wanted to hate because she had Augustus, but even then I could not hate her because she was a sweet person. I've never seen her yell or even say a vulgar word. She's different. She's pure. She doesn't deserve to know about the world Augustus has been informed of because it would taint her, take her away from what sets her apart. If she was a wolf, I would have no doubt that she would have Luna blood in her, for she would be the perfect Luna, strong and nice. Full of mercy and kindness. The perfect balance to a dominate Alpha.

Within ten minutes I am watching Molly hop into her car as I get into my own. She's worried for the boy that she loves and she's come to me because she knows that we were once best friends. I pull out of the driveway, heading down the familiar streets as I know the directions inside out. As I park my Prius right behind the familiar truck, I take in a deep breath, resting my head against the steering wheel. I prep myself, knowing that I am not only about to chat with the man I rejected, but with a human who has learned of a supernatural existence and is close to losing his mind like what the elders of our pack have always warned us.

"You can do this," I whisper, raising my head from the wheel as I open the door. Locking the car, I head for the front door, seeing the familiar window closed, the curtains pulled shut as a dim light can only be seen through a small crack. I know he will not be coming to the front door. Ringing the doorbell once, the familiar smile of a welcoming woman comes before me.

"Amory!" Mrs. Brown greets, welcome me inside the familiar house as she tells me how she hasn't seen me for quite some time. After a two minute chat, she tells me Augustus is up in his room. With Mrs. Brown heading back to her living room where she has a book on the couch open to a certain page. Heading up the stairs, I walk down the hallway to the familiar white door shut. Knowing it will be locked, I softly jump, grabbing the lock pick above his doorframe Augustus keeps since he commonly locks himself out on accident. Picking the lock, the door cracks open and I see a once organized room transform into an absolute mess. His bed unmade, books scattered in unorganized piles, empty sacks of food nowhere near the trash can overflowing wit energy drinks, the once perfectionist room is a complete mess.

"Augustus," I greet, only to find his headphones on and on max volume, his face illuminated by the light o his lab top as he looks up information on a source I've never seen regarding the werewolf world. "Augustus." I tap on his shoulder, barely even catching a hint of his attention. Right as I am about to tap again, his eyes widen and he falls out of his chair, scared as his fingers begin to shake. "Calm down." He pulls down the headphones, speechless as I hold out a hand to help him up. "We need to talk because Molly needs this. Not just Molly, but you. Your health and sanity needs this," I explain.

Augustus takes my hand hesitantly, up on his two feet as he backs up to the wall. "Your not even human. You're a damn wolf and a predator," he whispers, his voice shaky. "How the hell am I supposed to respond."

"You want answers about my world and I am here to give you with some amateur posting about it on some sketchy website." Pulling his hair up, I instruct Augustus to sit back down. As he steadily takes his seat, I shut his laptop, taking in a deep breath. "Ask away and I will reply."

"Are you a threat? Is your pack a threat to my life? To others lives?" He asks, searching my face as if looking for some off-putting detail.

"No. Unless you try and hurt us, we are harmless. We have our lives, just think of us like a type of religion. We have our goddess and our codes. We have our beliefs. But we are all living to get along with one another. As for those that could hurt you, think of them like your jail convicts, few in number and easy to contain." I just hope that made sense. I hope that I do not offend. I hope I do not frighten. "Think of us just as some community. One harmless and if anyone opposes a threat, there are individuals who take care of those threats just as you have your police."

"You mean hunters?" Augustus asks, placing his head in his hands as he takes in a shaky deep breath. "How am I supposed to live now. To think of Molly as having no threats when we go off to college. Excuse me for what I think of the supernatural world, but I don't want to even have kids knowing that the monsters parents tell their kids aren't true are actually quite real!" Augustus shoots up from his chair, frustrated as I see the dark circles under his eyes. "I worry for Molly. For us. For me. I worry that-

"Have you heard of a strange attack where someone gets the blood sucked dry out of them or someone gets mauled to death?" I ask, interrupting him as I keep my voice soft. "Show me the statistics of that."

His lips form a firm line and I briefly close my eyes to concentrate. "I understand. I understand how finding out about our world is a massive life changer and has affected you greatly, but believe me, Augustus, the only time a werewolf will attack you is if you try and attack them."

"What about all of this full moon shit?" He asks, pointing to a pile of scattered books that have diagrams of the moon, different phases and their effects upon the supernatural.

I shake my head. "The first world could only shift with the full moon, and as the first wolves begin to breed, the moon goddess watched as we populated the earth, some mating with other wolves and some with other creatures. A pure, pure wolf is rare and is often thought of as sacred. They shift only for the full moon. Common wolves that are practically all of us, we shift when we want and can control our wolf."

"But wolves are not the only concern," Augustus points out. I nod. "Vampires and witch? Fairies, dark creatures...all of these things are out there."

"And also have their own type of environment. Vampires and witches are in this hemisphere, but just like wolves, they are just as harmless. Fairies tend to be more towards the equator, elves tend to be in deep forests or places like Finland or New Zealand. The darker creatures are for the deep mountains and also parts of

Asia." Augustus nods, understanding more as I take a seat on his bed.

"Humans can scare us too just as we scare you, you know," I point out. "All through history there are greatly trained hunters that can do bad things, and these hunters don't just drive around in an Impala. We are scared of them, just as you are scared of us, the bunch of us supernaturals that are actually harmful."

"Can you promise me something?" I ask Augustus, rising to my feet as I head for the door. He nods, looking more sane than when I first arrived. "Go to Molly. She needs you and needs to know that you are okay and not insane. She is very worried and really does love you."

As Augustus makes that promise, I leave the house, heading for my car as I know that Augustus needed that talk, that it helped him. Sure, he will still be afraid and shocked, but he will always have our chat to remember when he feels afraid. He will always have that reassurance that he is safe, that Molly is safe, and that even his children one day will indeed be safe.

As my car comes to life and I back out of the driveway, I turn on the radio, tapping my fingers to the drums of the rock music as Flynn flashes through my mind. The man I love. The man I love with all of my heart. Images of his smile enter my mind, images of him laughing as a joke is told or I do something embarrassing. I remember him at the beach, how he did not fight Augustus because he knew he had to be the bigger person, that he respected not only me, but also Augustus. I remember him accepting his mates rejection as he walked over to me, as he held me in his arms. I remember the first and only night we have been together, how in the morning he was afraid that I was not pleased or if he was okay. He cares so much for me as do I for him. To think he started off as a friend in my opinion that I was too blinded by the mate bond to see was the true male I had been waiting for my whole life.

Arriving home, I place my keys on the counter, seeing a few texts from Flynn about the day as I head up my stairs. His last text was from two hours ago. Peeling off my clothes, I hop into the shower, cleansing myself as I hum a soft tune. As I hop out and put on my clothes for the evening, there's a knock. A knock at my window.

I head out of the bathroom, heading over to the mirror to see before me a beaten and bloody Flynn. His lip busted open, hash over his left eyebrow, his shoulder looking out of place, and a black eye, instincts flood my movements as I open the window, pulling him in as I cannot say any words.

I work fast, setting him onto my bed as he hisses in pain. Grabbing a face towel from the bathroom, I wet it down, applying it to his face as I inspect his every cut. Only, my eyes widen as I peel up his shirt, claw marks over his chest as my eyes begin to water and I watch his eyes close in pain.

Whoever did this to him, they are going to damn pay.

"Flynn," I cry, grabbing scissors as I find myself cutting away at his shirt to cause no pain, only to be mortified as I only find more gashes from claw and even bite marks. "Flynn, what happened?" I sob, covering my mouth as those hunter green eyes meet mine briefly.

"I'm free," he whispers, his voice weak as his head drops to the pillow.

I scream.

Chapter 30

I watch him, how his chest rises and falls peacefully as I run a stressful hand through my hair. With his blood cleaned up, his busted lip healing, his gashes still looking rough, black eye still making me worried, and his once dislocated shoulder back in place, I want to know what happened. What he meant by him finally being free. Placing my head down on the side of the bed, I lace my fingers with his, tears still forming as I still replay an hour ago in my head. My phone rings once more, my body too emotionally drained to even think about a social conversation as I just want to know if Flynn is okay. If he will wake up soon? Looking up, I rest my chin upon my hand, watching his hunter green eyes still shut as I just want to see them open. I just want to see him opening his eyes and a smile grace his face.

As the sun is gone, the moon out and bright tonight, I wipe away another tear, taking in every detail of his face. Taking ahold of my nerves, I gather myself to my feet, taking in a shaky deep breath as I become light-headed. "What are you free from?" I ask myself, thinking of all the possibilities. He's either a rogue because he told his father he did not want to be an Alpha, or he told his father he doesn't want to be Alpha and his father beat the shit out of him. "What are you free from?"

For the next two hours I sit beside Flynn, stressed beyond belief as my parents are just down the hall. They know of Flynn being here, of the bad state he is in, and how he does not want to be Alpha. My eyelids are heavier than ever, hard to stay awake as the hours take forever to go by. "Flynn," I whisper, my voice shaky as I rest my chin on my hand, close to his face as my eyes water. "Please be okay. I love you," I whisper, shutting my eyes as I find myself drifting off into a much needed sleep that I have tried to prolong. The moment I take in one last deep breath, I sense something. A movement.

My eyes peel open to see his fingers twitch, his pointer curl as his thumb does as well. He's waking up. Instantly I lace my fingers with his, jolting upright to meet his eyes that are barely open.

"Amory," he barely even is able to whisper, meeting my stare. I move fast, my hands cupping his face as I plant a soft kiss upon those lips. My heart fills with joy to see him awake. "Amory?" I nod, pulling back as he tries to sit up.

"What is it?" I ask, knowing that he's using much of his energy to just stay awake.

"I told my father that I love you..." He whispers, offering my a lopsided smile as I know he is in pain. "I told him he could fuck off and he listened as I told him I have no interests to be the next Alpha." That's why he's beaten. "He wants to make me a rogue and my mother has threatened to leave him if he does that."

I nod, watching as Flynn lays back down, grabbing my hand as he lightly tugs me closer. Once second I'm sitting beside him and shortly after I am beside Flynn, my face in a pillow as I close my eyes. He's asleep, needing his rest as I think of what is in store for Flynn. I cannot drift off into the awaiting arms of sleep, but rather my mind is filed with thoughts that act like a caffeine to my body. My tired body with a mind that is unable to calm itself down.

The sun rises as it will everyday, the sky filled with vibrant blues as I stretch out my arms. Knowing the bags under my eyes are present, they do not even compare to the signs of torment upon Flynn's body. As his chest rises and falls, my heart clenches as I see his torso bruised black and purple, small scabs now where the claw marks wounded him greatly. His face is busied and some dry blood still present as I push my self up into my elbows, looking at Flynn as I wonder what to do. Taking in a deep breath, I get out of bed, preparing for the day as I take a long shower, changing into old and comfy clothes as I still hear no movement from where Flynn lays. The second I step out of my bathroom, I'm surprised to find him sitting up, hissing in pain.

Instantly I run over to him, helping him sit up as my hands are careful where to press. "Advil?" I ask, taking his face in my hands as those beautiful green eyes connect with mine and my wolf does backflips. He doesn't say anything, rather pushing himself off of my bed as he towers over me. "Flynn?"

He shakes his head, heading for the bathroom I just exited, barely shutting the door as I let out a sigh. He's in pain. Hearing a cabinet open, I listen to the faucet run and a pill bottle being opened. I guess he found the Advil on his own. For another two minutes his is in there, leaving me isolated in the dead silence of my room as I worry what is running through his mind. "Flynn?" I call out, walking towards the door as I hear no movement.

He stands by the sink, fists white as he clenches the sink counter, his eyes turning black as he meets my gaze, and his whole body tended to the max. "Hey-

"My world is falling apart all around me, Amory," he interrupts, his tone sharp as he looks back to his reflection in the mirror. "I am watching my world fall to shit as my family faces a civil war and I know that no matter what happens, nothing can change the hate that is present in our family." My throat runs dry as Flynn shakes his head. "I've had my mind set on college since Olive died, knowing that I could be free from their presence as I was free to do whatever the hell I choose."

Flynn lets go of the counter, sliding down to the floor as he rests his back against the cold tile walls. "It's inevitable that my family is becoming just a show to the pack. The second my father declares me a rogue, my mother will leave him, and the pack will fall apart." Flynn has no desire to be Alpha, he hasn't for years. Olive was to be the Alpha and she died in a way that caused his father to become distant as he knew his son could never be enough. Alpha blood is strongest in the oldest child.

"You said you were free last night," I whisper, taking a seat on the floor across from Flynn. "What are you free from?"

He shakes his head, running a stressful hand through his hair. "I-" he pauses, pinching the bridge of his nose as my heartbeat speeds up faster than ever. "I made myself a rogue."

How? You have to be rejected by the Alpha to become a rogue. At least, that's the traditional way.

"How did you do that? I don't smell rogue on you," I input, raising an eyebrow as he lifts his left arm, right to where below his elbow, there's a small marking.

"After my father beat me, I ran, not because I was afraid, but because I knew how to settle the score." Where did he go? "Witches are not hard to find, and one happens to be in the area close by at a college." He takes in a deep breath, his shoulders relaxing. "The witch, Shay, simply helped me remove my ties to the pack." My eyes widen. "By the end of the day my scent will change." It means that by the end of the day, Flynn had better get his ass out of this town or the pack will kick him out of here. The Alpha will want him out of here and not even my parents will be able to disrespect him that much unless they too wis to leave the pack.

I shake my head. "Where are you going to go?" I ask, taking in a shaky deep breath. "We have three weeks till we leave for university. Where will you go?" I ask, my heart beginning to shatter as I know that where he goes, I cannot. I cannot just leave my family and pack behind, not because I am scared for going with Flynn, but because if I leave with him, I will be declared a rogue and that means Alpha Cade may even make my parents rogue.

Flynn scoots forward, grabbing my arms lightly as he pulls me into his embrace. With his chin resting atop of my head, his arms are wrapped around my small frame, holding me as if he has not done so for eons. "I love you, Amory," he whispers, placing a kiss upon my forehead as I nod. "I'm going go away for a little, Amory, just to get some space from everything." He needs space because of everything that has taken. Because he's decided to make himself rogue. Make himself rogue and he knows things will not go badly if he stays here in the territory of my pack. "I'm going to go away just to clear my mind."

I nod, pulling away a bit as my let a hand of my rest upon his face, cupping his cheek as his five o-clock shadow is present.

What do I even say to that? "Where? What if I need you, Flynn. What if something happens?" I ask, meeting his dark green eyes, his stare intense as my wolf slowly falls in submission to. It's the Alpha blood in his veins. I'm pushed lightly back to the wall, Flynn following as he leans in, his face buried in my neck as I close my eyes.

He's broken. He's in pain. Pain because every fiber of the pack is being stripped from him piece by piece. Flynn is needing me right now, for me to be beside him to pace the pain. To face the future actions as well of leaving to clear his mind.

I'm lifted up, arms wrapped around his neck as he carries me out of the room, holding me close as I can sense the weakness of his body still from last night. His arms shake every so often, trying hard to not drop me as his body is weak.

Set down upon bed, Flynn places his lips upon my own. Soft and slow, his kiss makes my world feel slow as time seems like nothing but an idea. As his hands travel to my shoulders, lightly pushing away as he parts with me. With my eyes still shut, I don't dare open them as I can feel his presence leave. I can hear the window open, Flynn leave as my eyes begin to water. I fall down to the floor, cold beneath me as I know Flynn needs to leave. Flynn needs to go before anything more can happen. His father will come looking for him, and he will come here first. Alpha Cade will be here soon, asking and bombarding me with questions as for where Flynn has gone.

And the second Alpha Cade sets foot into this house, all hell will break loose.

CHAPTER 31

"He's at the door," my mother informs, leaning against the doorway as I still sit on the floor where Flynn left just hours ago. Every ten minutes or so I'll find myself walks around the room, only to find myself back in the same location. Flynn left and he never told me where he went. Not because he's afraid I would tell, but because he knows that if I know the location, I would try and find him. Or that it's just best that I don't know. Don't know even though I have no idea how long he will be gone for. "He's enraged."

I expected that. I expected Alpha Cade to show up at our house and demand to speak with me. "Is Luna Willow with him?" I ask softly, watching as my mother nods her head. As long as Luna Willow is with the Alpha, I am okay with standing before the Alpha. I know what they will ask, how Alpha Cade will demand answers and say words that no Alpha should ever say to a pack member. Luna Willow will ask me calmly and politely, balancing out her husband as I know that I cannot give them the answers that they want. That I cannot because I do not know where Flynn has gone to. Gone to because he needs the escape, the peace, to make sure no more harm is done as he has become rogue.

Soon I will have to join him as well. As a rogue. As someone without their pack. Tradition says that the strength of the wolf is their pack, and no longer will that traditional belief apply to me. But then again, traditional beliefs have not always gone in my favor, as I have rejected my own mate and fallen in love with someone not my mate. Flynn's not my mate, there's no surprise involved in that, but the mate bond is merely a glue stick.

Getting to my feet, I grab a jacket, throwing it over my cold shoulders as I follow my mother out of the room and down the stairs. Already I can sense the tense atmosphere below in the living room, the silence as everyone has take their seats quietly, glares and glances the only form of communication as I find my vision beginning to blur. "Amory," Luna Willow greets, a forced smile upon her lips as I know she is dead worried. She holds nothing against me, but she wants my help to find her son and only child. She has already lost one child, and now, she has just lost another. Not lost like he will never return, but lost that he is now a rogue and stepping foot in our packs territory could mean severe punishment. "When did you last see Flynn?" She asks politely, watching as I take my seat, my parents leaving the room as Alpha Cade instructs them to do so. This is a conversation between the Alpha, Luna, and an average pack member who no one would ever think could be in this serious of a situation. Hell, in the yearbook I was voted most average. High school means everything to wolves, as it displays the foot chain for our kind, how the stronger become warriors or friends of the future Alpha, how they will hold higher ranks, and the nerds will most likely remain omegas or go off to college and never return back home.

"Four hours ago," I respond, trying to calm my nerves as I find my body not relaxed whatsoever. If anything, I feel like I'm being questioned in a police station for a murder. "He was here and left. He didn't tell me where he was going or doing," I inform, watching as Alpha Cade gets to his feet.

He shakes his head. "You're his whore, of course he would tell you," he snaps, only for Luna Willow to get to her feet, shaking her head as they hold a strong glare with one another. "He would tell her because he knows she will come when he wants to use her."

My throat becomes dry as I can feel my canines growing, pricking the surface of my lips as they wants to barge out and rip through his flesh. He has respected me too much already. "And you think treating her this way will get us closer to our son?!" Luna Willow snaps, her tone filled with sadness as I know she is suffering. "You are the one that has caused Flynn to do this, to run off. He is our only child, Cade. He is our only damn child and all you do is treat him like shit thinking he will stay!" Flynn doesn't want to be Alpha because he looks at his father everyday and does not want to become like him. He's told me this before, how he sees the Alpha position as a 'sign me up' for mental insanity. He's watched his family crumble and still have to be together, sewed together, just to put on a mask to the pack.

"It all started when Amory came along. The second he stood up to me was all because of her," Alpha Cade growls, his eyes turning black as I find mine as well becoming the dark color.

"Because he found someone worth sticking up for. Because he found someone who was beside him and not pressuring him, allowing him to be himself and pursue what he wants," I snap. "I didn't make your son stick up for himself, he made that decision, and I was there for moral support because no one else ever was."

I rise to my feet, eyes fixed upon the Alpha as I find my wolf coming closer to shifting. "Your son doesn't want to be Alpha because of me, because I came along, no! He doesn't want to be Alpha because not only does he have no want or dreams to be Alpha, but because he watches you. He sees you as a path he does not want to follow at all."

"Cade," Luna Willow snaps. "We are here to find our son, not argue about his decisions."

"What did he do last night?" Alpha Cade asks me, a small growl present as he is trying to contain his beast. "What did he say to you before he ran?"

"I would know," I snap, watching as Luna Willow raises an eyebrow. "Because the second he got here he passed out because you decided to beat the living shit out of him!"

Luna Willow looks to her husband, rage filling her eyes. "You did what?" She's mad. "You said you were taking care of business with a rogue last night. That was your response to the bloody knuckles."

I watch.

I watch as the Luna lands a hard punch to the Alpha's cheek, their marriage falling over like an unstable tower of Jenga blocks. She lands another hit to her husband, Alpha Cade not doing anything as I take a step back. Unstable. Sewed together. Their marriage is held together by a single string as two tons weigh gown upon it.

The Luna takes a step back, her hand covered in a bit of blood as I see she's broken her husband's nose. Taking in a deep breath, she looks back at her husband.

"The moment that we have Flynn back, Cade, I am going to reject you and let the whole pack know what a monster you are. I should of done this year's ago, I am only sad that I did not watch you walk out of my family's lift years ago."

The Luna heads for the door, leaving me speechless as I see her husband fuming mad. "If you dare lay a hand on Amory, Cade, I will send a hunter out on you."

Everything seems to happen so fast, how the head family of this pack has left my house, broken as I know that the pack will soon learn of what has been going on behind closed doors.

My parents are beside me in seconds, trying to have me listen to them, to explain things, but I don't. I head for the kitchen, grabbing my keys as I rush out of the house. I enter my car, making the engine come to life as I know I just need to get out of here. I just need some space and fresh hair. I need a place to think. I want Flynn by me, comforting me, hearing me out on how horrible I feel to have watched his whole family turn to a broken system.

I pick my destination, not knowing what to expect as I head for the front door. Knocking twice, I hear movement as I take in a shaky deep breath, tears forming as I don't know what to say. I don't know what to do. All I can think about is how the Luna punched her mate, how she told him she would reject him, how she looked broken as the truth finally was set free. I understand Flynn even more now on the basis of not wanting to be Alpha, how not only the Alpha is faced with pressures, but the Luna is too. The Luna is faced with the pressures of holding the family together even when it's broken. Even when it is a dead family until the string breaks and all must be unleashed to the people who looked up to them.

As the door opens, my vision blurs and the sounds are muffled. Someone says my name but I just stay focused on those bright green eyes. They ask me what I am doing here. I'm led up to the second floor, entering a room where the walls are pained a pastel purple. I'm given a place to sit as they hand me a glass of water. Months ago I would of never dreamed of coming here.

"Amory, are you okay?" Molly asks, concern filling her face as I meet her gaze. With my head held high, I know that I can no longer play the strong person. I have to let that mask drop.

"No," I whisper, my voice weak as I drop my chin and look to my fingers. "No I'm not."

Chapter 32

The sun is still bright, warm against my skin as we walk along the boardwalk. The wind is strong today, my hair pulled back into a bun to keep it from hitting my face and Molly's. Molly, a girl I've found myself around very much since two weeks ago. Two weeks ago when Flynn left, I saw his family fall apart, and I found my strength in confiding in her. Confiding in her not about the werewolf community, but I told her how Flynn is in a trough situation, so bad that he had to go away and his parents came to me. Came to me and I watched as they unraveled before my very eyes. Molly helped me, staying with me and comforting me. So for two weeks we have been having our, enjoying each other's company, laughing together as if best friends for years.

For tonight we are an hour away from our town, out on the boardwalk as there's also a bonfire at the beach tonight. With the bonfire just a little bit away, we are exploring the town, enjoying the one week the two of us have left until college. The one week left until I can see Flynn. Have I heard from him? Barely. He's told me he's taking time off and is just trying to figure things out. He called me a few times, saying he cannot chat long as every call he tells me that he loves me.

Luna Willow calls me everyday, asking if I know where Flynn is. I tell her the same everyday, that I do not know, that I am just as concerned as she is.

As for right now, Molly and I walk down the wooden stairs of the pier, the sand soon under my sandals. The group of thirty that we graduated with are just down the shore, the waves massive today as most of them have brought their surfboards. Once with the group, we partake in the activities, playing soccer along the shore, racket ball, and frisbee. Before long the sun begins to set, the pink and orange hues reflected in the ocean as the music begins and a few guys toss lighter fluid into the fire. I watch the flames go up immediately, how they seem to reach the sky, the bright colors illuminated off of others faces as I dance to the music. Grabbing a can of beer, I raise it to the sky, enjoying the time as I take a swing, handing some to Molly. I need this night, to have some fun, to try and escape the crisis surrounding me. No, Molly is not an escape, I genuinely enjoy her friendship and we are hitting it off pretty well, but I still want Flynn with me.

Soon the moon is up, the few other wolves in this group all feeling even more alive as the moon calls to us. As the tide comes in, I grab a surfboard, heading out with some other guys as we head for the deep. The deep where the monsters lurk, where the creatures stay below the surface, awaiting the prey to become stupid and tread in the deep. Where the lamb trespasses into the lions territory. It's where Flynn is right now, treading in the deep end as his family places impossible pressures upon him. His father the monster that lurks for him, the pressures of Alpha lurking after him, and so much pressure that if he doesn't escape the tide, he will be lost. That's why Flynn is gone right now, he needs to think on his own. I pray to the Moon Goddess. I actually partake in the old religion of the werewolf kingdom when the tradition of prayer was highly important. There was once a time where the Priestesses of the Temples were the true leaders of the werewolf kingdom and we were to pray. I've prayed for the past two weeks for Flynn, for him to be safe, for him to come back home.

But what is Flynn's home? Not with his parents. Not while his father is there. Not his pack, not when they expect him to lead them for the next many years.

"Amory," someone calls motioning to the wave approaching as I get ready to ride it. As the wave comes, I push off, riding the wave easily back to the shore as I let the wave fall over me in the end. As the water envelops me, I listen to the beating of my heart, trying to calm my mind as I resurface. Taking in a deep breath, I open my eyes, pushing my hair back as I look to the shore.

It feels like I'm in a trance as the moonlight shines upon me, how I feel like I am just stuck in a trance. In a routine. I head back to where the group is again, waiting another wave as I spot Molly by the shore, running with wide arms to where Augustus is. He planned to be here after all. As I watch the two of them, I feel jealous, not because this time I hate Molly because she has Augustus, but because I want that. I want that to be me right now, with Flynn, greeting him after two weeks of his departure. I want to see him, to see his smile, to hold him close, even if just a hug. I miss him more than I ever missed Augustus. More than I ever wanted Augustus when he was Molly's.

I don't pay attention, a wave crashing over me as I'm taken down. Water fills my nose, the salt water slightly burning my eyes before I can shut them, and wanting to only resurface. I pull myself up, taking in a deep breath, only for another water to crash as I find myself struggling this time to fight the current.

Panic.

The current is strong, pulling me down deeper to where the creatures lurk.

I resurface, taking in a massive breath of air, my heart racing as I find myself back and grabbing onto my board, holding onto it. I shut my eyes tightly, reopening them to find myself a little off from the group I was with, a short swim back to shore. Placing myself back upon the board, I swim to the shore, the sand soon beneath my feet as I take off the strap to the board. I'm also lucky that my top stayed tied up, the burgundy top somehow having stayed up and making me feel at least a tad refreshed. Walking back to the party, I join back into the dancing, trying to forget what just happened as I throw my hands up into the air and move my body.

Someone comes up behind me. I push them away, moving closer to the center where the most people are located. Closing my eyes, I let my head fall back slightly, enjoying the beat of the music as it vibrates in my body.

In a little I'm back near the drinks, grabbing another beer can as I look out upon the ocean. Taking my drink, I walk a little way down the shore, the waves brushing against my ankles as I take a seat on the sand. Building little towers, I take a swing at my drink, enjoying the isolation out here as those green eyes flash through my mind. I miss him so much.

Laying down, I take in a deep breath, hearing someone walk to where I am. Maybe Molly?

Opening my eyes, they go wide, my body feeling as if in a dream as I get to my feet. Dropping my drink, I walk, my pace quickening as I run over, my pace getting faster with every step as his do as well. I watch as those arms stretch open, my knees bending as I push off, wrapping my legs around his waist as I cannot get rid of the smile upon my face. I place my lips against his, pulling him close as he falls lightly into the sand, me on top as I do not want to let go.

Hunter green eyes. Beautiful green eyes that long eyelashes frame. I take in every aspect of his face as I pull away, his slightly crooked nose, tanned skin, jawline, high cheekbones, the very light dusting of freckles upon his nose and cheeks. I run my hands through his hair, the messy and dark hair as I watch the smile spread across his face as my heart does a backflip.

He's here. He's with me. He's in my embrace as I am in his as well.

"Flynn," I whisper, my eyes beginning to water up as I see the same emotions within his own eyes. "Goddess I've missed you." He sits up, wrapping his arms around my smaller frame as I burry my face in his neck. A sob escapes my lips, so happy to see him. "Goddess knows that I have fucking missed you." He pulls back, placing his lips upon my own as I close my eyes, his hands cupping my cheeks, a smile forming upon his lips as my wolf bounces off the walls.

"Amory?"

I pull back, looking into those eyes that I have missed for two weeks. "Yes?"

"I've missed you so much," he informs, his eyes searching my face, as if taking in every detail as he has not seen it for two weeks. Two weeks since he turned rogue and I can smell it on him. The smell every rogue holds, but I'm not affected. Not affected because I've missed him, wanted him, needed him. Love him so much that I do not give a damn if his scent is off. "I made up my mind upon my mother," he explains. I had told him about what his parents had to say not only to me, but each other, that night I saw everything going totally bitter. "I am going to tell my mother about my decisions, but I will not talk with my father."

We both know that the second he tells his mother what is going on, his mother will let the pack know what has been going on. We both know how the pack will respond will only result in Alpha Cade being seen as someone no longer as a figurehead. Most likely they will force him out of the pack.

"Are you going to return or stay away still? It's only a week."

He rests his forehead upon mine, holding me close. "I'm going to meet my mother before I leave. I'll be gone for another week and the day we have tickets to move to college, I'll go to my mother and inform her," Flynn responds, taking in a deep breath. "Did you know I looked up what your name meant after prom night?" I raise an eyebrow. "It was prom that I realized how broken you were. All night I thought about what you were in, what I would of done if in your shoes. I decided to look up your name, just interested in it."

"What did you find?" I ask, my voice soft as I recall the day my mother explained to me why she named me Amory.

"It means lovely in French," he answers, a ghost smile tugging at his lips. "It's the perfect name for you, the only one that could ever describe you."

Mother told me that she wants my name to represent the beauty between father and her, how it is a beautiful marriage. She told me how the first time she looked into my eyes, I struck her as the most precious and beautiful thing that she had ever set eyes upon.

"Amory?"

"Yah?" I ask, meeting his soft gaze as my body seems to relax.

"I want to let you know that I will be back by the end of the week, to tell my mother about what is happening." He's leaving again. But he will be back. But he will be gone. "I love you, but I have to go again."

I look back to the party taking place quite a ways away. Looking back to Flynn, I tilt my head to the side. "Not yet, right?" I ask kindly, a smirk tugging at the corner of my lips. Flynn shakes his head 'no,' letting me know we still have time left until we have to part again. I place my lips upon his, pushing the two of us back to the sand as the moonlight is bright tonight, shining upon the sand as it causes the grains to appear like diamonds.

CHAPTER 33

I watch him, how he looks rough. His black hair unruly, in every direction as anyone could tell he hasn't bothered to brush it for days. His clothing is different, no longer just a worn t-shirt or sweats, but rather a pair of combat boots and a flannel. He looks rough. My eyes follow his every movement, watching as he walks up to the door. My parents could smell the rogue scent on him the moment he parked his car on our driveway. Unlike many who would see Flynn and immediately want to harm him, a smile spreads across my face, my fingers gripping the handle of my luggage as my father is outside loading his car.

I watch as Flynn walks to my father outside, offering him a welcome smile as I watch my father not respond how I would expect him to. With the last luggage for the airport in my presence, I let go of it, heading for the mirror as I watch my father not just shake hands with Flynn, but pull him in for one of those 'bro-hugs' where Anton can tell it is one of respect and almost like an acceptance of family. With my mother beside me, I can tell she is also surprised, slightly gasping as I reach for the door handle.

The moment that they stand apart from one another, I run, the door swinging open as his eyes meet my own. I throw myself at him, wrapping my arms around his neck as he swings me around twice. Am I happy? Is it not obvious. As my feet touch he ground, I look to Flynn, what I already want to ask already about to be answered as he parts his lips. "I told her about my decision," he comments, wrapping an arm over my shoulder as I nod, worried about how Luna Willow took it.

"Flynn," my mother calls from the front door as I watch as a neighbor's door opens up. They can smell Flynn's rogue scent and it only means judgement upon my family's name. "Come on in, don't be a stranger, we are just loading a few of Amory's luggages."

Flynn smiles, walking with me to my mother as she stands in the doorway, awaiting us as my father follows. Already it seems as if they are treating him like a son or boyfriend...unlike the rest of the pack could ever as long as he holds the rogue scent.

The second we enter our house, my mother offers Flynn some lunch. As Flynn enters the kitchen, I give my father the last luggage, overhearing how my mother asks how Flynn is doing. Within ten minutes Flynn is following me up the stairs, looking at all the pictures lining the walls, each of me growing up that can cause me to become deeply embarrassed. The moment that I open my bedroom door, Flynn places his lips upon mine, lightly pushing me up against the wall as I run my fingers through his tangled black locks.

"What happened?" I ask, breathless as Flynn pulls away, his lips brushing across my collarbone. "How did you mom respond?"

He takes in a deep breath, pulling away as I expect bad news, only for a soft smile to trace his lips. "She said that she understood.

She also told me that she has kicked my father out of the house and will be telling the pack tomorrow night at a pack dinner about their Alpha." I'm shocked. Alpha Cade is out of the house and the pack will be informed about his behavior. "She also says that the pack doors are always open to me."

"I am relieved," I comment, happy that the Luna has taken these massive steps. Taking my fingers from his locks, I let a soft laugh escape my lips. "You may want to take a shower before our plane leaves." Flynn nods, smiling at my remark as he agrees. It seems like he hasn't showered for a few days. Though I will say, the five o-clock shadow upon his face does not just make him look a bit more mature, but also sexy.

Within twenty minutes Flynn stands beside me as we watch my car prepared for the trip to the airport. With my parents just grabbing a few objects from the house, there's a countdown until my departure. But if this were a different story, I would be leaving Flynn behind, waving goodbye as I would know I would not be able to see him for a while. But this is my story.

This is our story.

One where Flynn's car is packed up as well, my mother with his extra set of keys to drive it back to his house once we depart. One where Flynn and I have seats right next to one another for a flight that takes us to the same destination. With my fingers interlaced with his, I rest my head upon his shoulder, looking to the silent street as the sun is still bright.

"You know we are two damn lucky people, right?" I ask, lifting my head from his shoulder as I meet his eyes. "Damn lucky to have found one another in a world where traditional tries to tell us how to love or lives and some people need to be able to pick their own destiny." Flynn smiles softly at me, kissing my forehead. "Damn lucky that we have come this far and a whole future awaits the two of us."

"You know that I have to be the luckiest guy alive right now because I have you, right?" I smile, wrapping my arms around him for a short embrace as my parents walk out. "Ready?" Flynn asks, watching as I nod, the two of us waving bye to my parents as we head for his sleek car. I remember the first time we drove together, how he demanded I move over to the passenger seat because he didn't want me to drive in the state that I was in. I remember how I discovered his taste in music, how I found myself listening to that music just because I was beginning to fall hard for him. It took me too long to notice, but maybe it was good for me to have been blind for so long? Maybe it was good that he had to show me that we could be good together. That we would become great together. He stole my heart as I stole his.

So here I sit, that same song playing, the tow of us singing to the song, Flynn taking his fingers to the beat, me mimicking the classic rock's guitar solo, and the two of us in love.

The closer the airport gets, the more nervous I become. But I should not be. Not completely. Why? Because I have Flynn beside me for the bumpy road ahead as he has me as well. "Amory?" I turn to face Flynn, watching as he takes ahold of one of my hands and places it into his lap. "My mother told me something that I want to pass onto you." I await. He smiles. "She told me she's sad I do not want to be Alpha not just because I would not become Alpha, but because you would not be Luna. She told me that the moment she saw you stand up to my father, she wanted you to be the Luna. Only you." Luna Willow respects me. She trusts me. She not only wants me to be the next Luna, but this shows that she sees Flynn and I as husband and wife, as any Luna and Alpha are. She basically just wished for us to get married as well.

As the airport is before us, we get ready. With luggage out, I help Flynn unload his massive luggages for the next year ahead. Just as he shuts the trunk, my mother pulls me in for a long hug. "My baby Amory," she softly cries, holding me close as I feel the tears coming from me as well. "You've grown up so fast and I am so sad to see you go." I hold her close as I thank her for all she has done. I watch as my father walks up to Flynn, telling him to always be there for me. To always be beside me in my ups and downs.

As my mother pulls back and my father pulls me in for a big hug, the water works begin, both tears of sadness and happiness as I know the next chapter of my life will be only bright. Bright because of the boy beside me.

Within ten minutes I watch as my parents drive off, Flynn pulling me in for a hug as I let out a shaky sob, sad to see them go as I won't see them till Thanksgiving Break. As Flynn and I head in for baggage check and our tickets, we turn around, hearing our names called out as I watch her blond hair fly in the wind. I've never seen her run, never even imagined in those lavender heels that she wears. "Flynn! Amory!" I watch as Luna Willow runs to us, a few cars honking at her as she simply just ignores them. "Don't you two leave without me saying my goodbye!"

Flynn lets go of my hand, running to his mother as he pulls her in for a big embrace. "Don't you dare forget your mother," Luna Willow cries, lightly laughing as she issues her son's cheek. "And Amory." I look to meet her eyes, watching as she motions for me to come forward. Making my way to the Luna as the workers take our luggage to be loaded, I find myself in the embrace of the Luna, her tears wetting my cheek as she holds me close. "Don't you dare hurt my son," she whispers into my ear playfully. "Because I want to see my grandchildren have your features." I smile at her remark, my heart warm as Flynn informs us that our plane leaves soon.

Luna Willow lets go, telling me to be careful as she goes back to her son. "I love you, sweetie, don't get that because you will always have your childhood room awaiting you."

As the Luna waves goodbye to us, we head beyond the security checkpoint, hand in hand for our gate as our plane will soon leave. Once we take our seats, I let out a deep breath, smiling as Flynn rests his head on my shoulder. "You know we have another four years before us," he starts off, the two of us waiting for the plane to be ready to load. "Four years for countless things to happen, and maybe even more years after that." My checks become tinted with pink. "What shall we do first to tell our children about?"

My heart skips a beat and a ghost smile crosses my face. Children. Could I have children with Flynn? There's no doubt about it. About my love for him. About how I would love to start a family with him and raise children under our own house's roof.

As our plane is called to be loaded, we rise, ready for our next adventure together. With the two of us excited for the next four years, we know that it holds only good memories as we have each other. Just the two of us.

Just the two of us is all that we need.

Epilogue

He was never mine. He could never be mine. I know that now, I've known that for four years now. After all, all it took was one simple act of intimacy and he had fallen head over heels for me. All it took was one simple act of intimacy and I soon learned the truth about how mates function. I learned that the mate bond did not make you in love with your mate, but with the idea.

I understand that. I understand that destiny is not what people make it out to be. It's your choice that is important, not destiny.

I watch him, the small girl by his side, her hand in his, her blond curls and bright green eyes. She has her mother's eyes and her father's hair. As I look at the small child, I see that if I had believed in destiny, she would not be here today. He looks happy as she walks beside him, a bright pink bow in her hair as her father looks to the woman beside him. His places a soft kiss upon his wife's cheek, her red hair pulled back, her bright green eyes causing me to think back to the night I saw them first kiss. The nights I watched in agony as my true soul mate was feet apart from me.

Everything worked out well in the end, how I now sit in the booth of this family-owned restaurant. How I now sit watching a family I could of made disappear if I was stupid in following traditions. All it took was for me to see how blind I was, how Augustus May of been the perfect boy in my mind at the time, but he was never my perfect match. I see that now, how Molly was his perfect match, how they look at one another with pure love that could warm any icy heart.

Augustus thanked me in the end. On his wedding day he thanked me for all I had done for his life. I remember rejecting him, how he found out about the supernatural. I never wanted him to know what I was, afraid he could not keep a secret. Afraid he would never want to see me again. He was afraid, submerging himself in a world that not many are used to. He told me how he did not want to raise a family in a world where monsters lurked, but I proved him wrong on what the definition of monster was. I show him that our world was one to not be afraid of, that I was someone to be trusted even if I was what he once called a monster. Now he raises his daughter knowing about a world of creatures so few even have beliefs about.

To him I am not just the shy girl he saw one day at school who he became best friends with. To him I am no longer just the best friend through high school that created beautiful memories that still cause me to smile today. To him I am the godmother to his daughter and his wife's Maid of Honor. I had patched things up with them that summer before college. Molly became my rock while Flynn was gone and taking a break from the pressures of his family. As Molly and I became good friends, soon enough Augustus and I fixed those tears in our friendship. After all those years, Molly has become one of my best friends and Augustus is still my best friend. In the end, we are all still linked together, putting the bitter parts of our memories behind us as we still smile and make memories that we are proud of.

They cross the street, coming to dinner with me as I hold the envelope in my hands. The envelope that holds such an importance to me that I had to just call them up and invite them to a dinner. As the bell rings once the door opens, I rise to my feet, waving to Augustus, Molly, and Quinn. Quinn waves back, the three year old letting a bright smile appear on her face as she runs over to me. Last Christmas I had enjoyed Christmas Eve a bi with them, spending much time with their daughter as she told me I was one of her best friends. Augustus now raises their daughter with who he once thought was a monster because of what I am. He raises his daughter with a werewolf as her godmother.

"Amory, how are you?" Molly asks, pulling me in for a hug as Augustus helps his daughter into a seat. "What is this big news about?"

I had flown in from Colorado to see them, to visit and tell them the news back home. Back here to bring them news of something big and exciting for everyone I hold dear to me. My parents discovered last night at a game night in my childhood house.

"And where is your husband?" Augustus asks, looking around as I twirl the ring around on my finger. I married a computer programmer two years ago while in my sophomore year of university. I married my soul mate and I've never look back. I've never been happier either.

"Where's Uncle Flynn?" Quinn asks, looking around for Flynn, the man I married. He proposed out of the blue one night, after a stressful week of finals in his dorm. With a blizzard having moved in, I found myself in his apartment, cold and tired from the storm. We were taking shelter from the winter cold and he got down onto one knee, tears spilling from my eyes, and his love infinite. He asked me to marry him simply, nothing fancy or ostentatious, he got down onto one knee and told me words that no poet could ever recreate.

"He forgot his phone in our car," I explain. I married a man with Alpha blood. I watched as my husband rejected the life of an Alpha because he did not believe in destiny, but making his own choices. He deemed himself a rogue after his father threatened to do so, a father who he forgave but has not seen for four years. Alpha Cade was rejected by his own people, the pack agreeing without any disagreement on his rejection and for his Luna to take the title of Alpha. Now the Luna is the Alpha, running our pack strong as she still welcomes us back as her family. The pack has never been stronger nor has ever felt like such a family. Their doors are still open to us, but Flynn and I are both rogues, enjoying the freedom as I know we both have no desire to take up the responsibilities that are still open to us back here. For now we live life in the mountains of Colorado, enjoying the freedom and human realm as we know that one day we may have to take up those roles.

"What is the news?"

The door rings, my heart skipping a beat as I meet those hunter green eyes. He runs a hand through his black locks, smiling my way as Molly and Augustus greet him with smiles. "Did you tell them?" He asks, pulling me in for a side hug as he places a kiss upon my forehead. I feel perfectly placed within his embrace, as of the Moon Goddess made him just for me and I just for him.

"I was waiting for you," I explain, handing Molly and Augustus over the envelope. Pride swells in my heart and I can tell Flynn is excited for their reaction, how he straightens his posture and holds me closer.

Their eyes widen.

"Are you serious?" Molly gasps, looking my way, looking me up and down as Flynn smiles. He's proud. Hell, his coworkers tell me he reminds them everyday. The moment we found out he called his mom and informed her, crying on the phone as he said that he loved me so much.

"Three months serious," Flynn comments, holding me even closer as they look at the sonogram of our child. Our child. Our family. Soon there will be a mini Flynn or Amory running across the floors of our house. Soon we will have a family, a child to raise as year's lay before us for that happiness.

We take our seats, chatter filling the air as we talk our way through the evening. Flynn takes ahold of my hand, squeezing it softly as I don't need to remind myself that I am happy. I don't need a reminder anymore, because I wake up every day and the first thing I see are beautiful hunter green eyes that hold so much love in them I could swear I am reliving our wedding day. Every morning I wake up to a soft kiss and him telling me that he loves me while every night the last thing I see are his eyes.

All is well because I did not let one act of intimacy mark my destiny. All is well because I said screw destiny and tradition, because I made my choice and my choice was not a glue stick, but superglue.